"Thank you for

Ruth squatted down and addressed Lucas. "Be a good boy for your daddy, okay? No running into roads."

"Ja gut," replied the little boy. He smiled and abruptly threw his arms around the woman. She hugged him tight, and he saw her eyes close as she rocked the boy ever so slightly.

For some reason Adam's throat closed up. There was something about the gesture that reminded him of his wife.

He took his son's hand and returned to the buggy.

"I like her," Lucas pronounced as Adam swung the buggy toward home.

"She seems nice," he affirmed. "I hope she can get her car fixed."

She had offered her services as a nanny. What a pity she wouldn't be around long enough for that to come to pass.

The truth of the matter was, he could use a nanny. Badly. Lucas was an impulsive child, without a mother's guiding hand, and Adam had a business to run.

What he needed, of course, was a wife. But in the meantime, a nanny might do.

Living on a remote self-sufficient homestead in North Idaho, **Patrice Lewis** is a Christian wife, mother, author, blogger, columnist and speaker. She has practiced and written about rural subjects for almost thirty years. When she isn't writing, Patrice enjoys self-sufficiency projects, such as animal husbandry, small-scale dairy production, gardening, food preservation and canning, and homeschooling. She and her husband have been married since 1990 and have two daughters.

Books by Patrice Lewis

Love Inspired

The Amish Newcomer
Amish Baby Lessons
Her Path to Redemption
The Amish Animal Doctor
The Mysterious Amish Nanny

Visit the Author Profile page at LoveInspired.com.

The Mysterious Amish Nanny

Patrice Lewis

LOVE INSPIRED

INSPIRATIONAL ROMANCE

LOVE INSPIRED®

INSPIRATIONAL ROMANCE

Recycling programs
for this product may
not exist in your area.

ISBN-13: 978-1-335-58543-1

The Mysterious Amish Nanny

Love Inspired
22 Adelaide St. West, 41st Floor
Toronto, Ontario M5H 4E3, Canada
www.LoveInspired.com

Printed in U.S.A.

For I was envious at the foolish,
when I saw the prosperity of the wicked.
—*Psalm* 73:3

To God, for blessing me with my husband and daughters, the best family anyone could hope for.

Chapter One

Well, if she had to be stranded in the middle of nowhere, at least the scenery was nice.

Ruth Wengerd gazed at the high snow-capped mountains visible over the tops of the conifers that lined this lonely stretch of two-lane road in western Montana. Here in early September, the grasses were yellow and dry, but the air was fresh and crisp. She almost fancied she could smell apples alongside the scent of pine. Glancing across the road, she saw a gnarled tree with small green fruits. Wild apples, from the look of it.

She peered at the underside of her vehicle. She'd stopped driving and pulled over half an hour ago, after hearing a loud, terrifying *klonk* followed by a horrific rhythmic banging under her car. Something beneath the chassis had given way, and she had no mechanical knowledge of what it could be. Now she didn't dare drive further.

She huffed out a breath of annoyance and slumped against the car. She couldn't even call for roadside assistance. After limping to this little apron off the road, she'd belatedly realized she'd left her cell phone at the last rest stop a hundred miles ago. She hadn't thought of it until she'd reached for it after the clang had forced her to pull over.

So here she was, two thousand miles away from the job she'd fled, and fifteen hundred miles away from her foster parents. Why had she chosen to travel this seldom-used road instead of staying on the highway? How far away was she from any chance of a tow truck? And was she the only person to travel this road? She'd been here thirty minutes already and not one vehicle had passed by. The sun was getting lower in the sky, and she wondered how cool the nights were around here.

"Idiot," she berated herself. Her foster father had cautioned her about her impetuous nature. As always, he was proved right. She had hastily left her job and her apartment in New York City after her disastrous decisions had resulted in massive financial losses for both herself and her clients.

Now that same impulsivity had resulted in her being stranded out in the middle of nowhere. Ruth kicked at a tuft of grass and wondered how she could have been so stupid as to leave her phone behind.

Fifteen more minutes passed. Ruth couldn't help but appreciate the sweet air and birdsong, even as she continued to stew over her situation.

Then, faintly in the distance, she heard a clip-clop of horse hooves. Her memory flashed back to her childhood in Pennsylvania, with its ubiquitous sound of the horse-drawn Amish buggies. But of course there were no Amish buggies out here in the wilds of Montana. She smiled at her folly.

But the sound persisted and grew louder. Finally, around a bend in the road, she saw…an Amish buggy. It was drawn by a horse with a glossy brown coat and guided by a man in a straw hat with a small boy next to him. She saw a yellow Labrador retriever sitting behind the child.

Her jaw dropped . What on earth was this man and his buggy doing in Montana?

The man slumped in his seat, the reins held loosely in his hands. He seemed not to notice her at first. But suddenly he raised his head and she watched him straighten up and re-grip the reins.

She lifted a hand in greeting and he returned the gesture. As he approached, he slowed the horse and pulled the animal to a stop.

"I'm so glad to see you!" she exclaimed. "No one's come by for ages. Is there a town nearby? I'm stranded."

"I can take you into town," the man said with an easy smile. She saw the ripple of muscle under his shirt. A working man. He had curly brown hair barely visible under the straw hat. His blue eyes crinkled. He was also clean-shaven. Ruth remembered Amish men had beards after they married, so she wondered if the child was not his. The boy, wearing a miniaturized straw hat over blond curls, regarded her with large curious brown eyes. He wore a dark blue shirt.

"Thank you," she said. She turned to collect her purse from the car.

Suddenly she heard the child shout something. The

next thing she knew, the yellow Lab had leaped from the buggy and was cavorting over to her. The animal reared up on his hind legs, smiling and panting. His whole body wiggled in excitement at meeting a stranger.

"Hey, there, buddy, calm down." She laughed, petting the rambunctious dog.

"Lucas, *nee*!" the man called sharply as the child suddenly jumped down after the dog.

Then, to complicate the situation, a car abruptly roared around the bend in the road. Seeing the buggy stopped in the middle of the lane, it honked its horn, scaring the horse.

The Amish man had his hands full controlling the animal. The dog looked ready to run away in panic, with the child straining after him. Gasping in fear, Ruth instinctively grabbed both the dog's collar and the boy's shirt, holding them in place until the car sped past, the driver shaking a fist out the window in anger.

Just as suddenly, all was peaceful again. Birds sang. A small flock of geese flew overhead. Frogs croaked in a distant ditch. It had all happened so fast it was hard to grasp how quickly the situation could have turned disastrous. Ruth's hands shook from adrenaline.

The man soothed the horse, applied the brake on the buggy and vaulted out of the seat. His face was dark as a thundercloud as he strode toward the boy and began scolding him.

Listening, Ruth roughly comprehended the dialect. She had heard—much less spoken—very little Pennsylvania Dutch since she was eleven and her parents had died, but the man's angry words pierced the filter of time in her brain and made sense.

The child looked shamefaced. Ruth, who had continued to grip the dog's collar, relaxed her hold on him.

Summoning up the reserves of the language in her memory, she said in halting German, "Too bad the road isn't wide enough for buggies."

The man's head snapped up. She saw conflicting emotions on his face—surprise at her use of German mingled with lingering anger at his son's impulsive actions.

He stared at her a few moments, then said in English, "You speak our language?"

"Not for a long time," she explained. "I was raised Amish until I was eleven years old. I haven't spoken much *Deutsch* since then."

A glimmer of humor crossed his face. "Then you understood the tongue-lashing I just gave Lucas."

"Most of it," she admitted. She dropped to one knee to look the boy in the eyes. "Do you speak English?" she asked him.

The child nodded.

"Then you understand why it was dangerous to nearly run in front of the car, right?"

"Ja," the child responded. "I'm sorry."

She had to resist the urge to hug him. There was something lovable about the boy's wide brown eyes and blond curls.

She rose to her feet in time to see the man wipe a hand across his face. "That could have been a very bad situation," he murmured. He met her eyes. "I have much to thank you for. You saved both my son and our dog from being hit by that car."

"Which was driving way too fast," she confirmed.

He stuck out a hand. "My name is Adam Chupp," he said. "And this is my four-year-old son, Lucas."

She shook his hand. "Ruth Wengerd. Thank you for stopping. Something broke on the underside of my car and I'm stranded here. To make matters worse, I accidentally left my phone at a rest stop outside of Great Falls, so I couldn't even call for a tow truck."

"I can take you into town." He rubbed his beardless chin. "It's a small town, but I would guess there's a tow truck service there. Meanwhile, if you have a suitcase or something, you might want to bring it along, since it's getting late."

She opened the back door of her car and extracted a small suitcase. She wondered briefly if there was anything else of value she should bring with her, and decided there wasn't.

Adam took the suitcase and swung it into the back of the buggy. Next, he bent down to first lift the dog, then Lucas up. He walked around to the driver's side, paused a moment to pat the horse on the neck and speak a couple of low words to it, then hoisted himself into the seat.

Ruth also climbed into the buggy. It amazed her that she still remembered how to enter the vehicle with any grace in a skirt. And she never wore anything but skirts, a lingering legacy from the modest dress of her youth.

The buggy was cramped with three people in front and the dog wagging in back. "Will you sit on my lap?" she asked the boy in German. Silently he nodded, and she lifted the child across her knees as Adam clucked to the horse.

"It's been a long time since I've traveled by buggy," she remarked. The scenery was immediately a much more intimate part of the journey, rather than whizzing by a window, barely glimpsed. She could savor the sweet smell of the pines and admire the mountaintops visible over the trees.

"It's unusual to find an *Englisch* woman who was raised Amish," the man remarked. "Where are you from?"

"Originally from Pennsylvania. My parents left the church when I was eleven years old, but they died in a car accident shortly after."

He winced. "I'm sorry. That must have been very difficult for you."

"It was." She was silent a moment, feeling the trusting warmth of the child in her arms, remembering the tragedies of her youth. "I don't think my father ever quite grasped the science of driving a car in the same way as someone who grew up around them. But I must say, it's nice to be in a buggy again."

Adam found himself full of questions about this strange woman he'd found stranded, but it would be rude to grill her minutes after meeting her. She had something of an impish look about her—slim, a bit sloppy, with long brown hair braided down her back and luminous brown eyes. Her skirt and blouse had a rumpled look to them.

Why did her parents leave the Amish? It was unusual

for adults to leave the church. But he wasn't likely to find out. He would drop her off in town, she would call a tow truck, her vehicle would get repaired, and she would be on her way.

On her way...

Suddenly it dawned on him he had no idea of her destination. "Where are you going?" he asked her. "I hope you won't be late for something. It must be very inconvenient to have your vehicle break down out here. This is a very rural part of Montana."

"So I noticed." She smiled. "I don't have a particular destination in mind. I was just taking a—a cross-country trip."

Her words seemed both hesitant and evasive. "So you won't miss any important appointment by being delayed a day or two?" he persisted.

"No. I'm afraid to find out what it will cost to get my car fixed, though. Whatever happened sounded pretty dire—a huge bang and clatter, like something fell off or broke apart."

"*Ja*, that doesn't sound good." He considered a moment. "There is a motel in town. There is also a boardinghouse in town run by some people in our church. They rent rooms. I can drop you off at either location."

"A boardinghouse, huh?" The woman rubbed her chin thoughtfully. "I've been staying in a series of cheap motels for the last couple of weeks. An Amish-run boardinghouse sounds like a nice change."

If she'd been traveling for days, that would explain the creased clothing. "It's very basic," he warned, "but clean as a whistle, and the people who run it are very nice. It's also less expensive than the motel."

"So how is it there's an Amish church this far West? I don't think I recall ever hearing about Amish in Montana."

"We are a fairly new settlement," he explained. "Most of us come from Indiana, but there's a smattering from Ohio and Pennsylvania and a few other states. It was just getting too crowded in the Midwest, and farmland was getting too expensive. A huge ranch came up for sale outside the town of Pierce—that's where we're headed, by the way—and our church bought it and is parceling it out to church members. Pierce is a small town, about twenty-five hundred people. But because it's so isolated, it has many amenities—a small hospital, grocery store, veterinary clinic, that kind of thing."

"And hopefully a mechanic." She grinned.

He grinned back. Her dark eyes sparkled with mirth. She seemed like something of a silly woman—frivolous, unprepared—but somehow endearing. "*Ja*, I think there's a mechanic. Several, in fact."

"Sounds like a nice little town."

"It is." He paused for a moment. "And one of the unexpected side effects of moving a church out here is how many people came for a fresh start, leaving painful things behind." The moment the words were out of his mouth, he wanted to snatch them back. What an awkward thing to say to a stranger.

Sure enough, the woman shot him a look. "Painful things? Does that include you?"

He blew out a breath and kept his explanation as brief

as possible. "*Ja*. My wife passed away when Lucas was a baby. It was hard to stay in a place where everything reminded me of her. I thought moving here would give me a chance for a new beginning."

He saw her nod, but to his relief she didn't ask any more questions about his past. He did, however, see her arms tighten fractionally around the child in a protective gesture. The tiny movement warmed him. Clearly, she was a woman who liked children.

"Well, if you're looking for a nanny, let me know," she said in a half-joking tone. "It looks like I'll be needing a job to pay for car repairs."

He was startled. He honestly hadn't considered that possibility at all—to find someone who could care for Lucas full-time rather than the series of teenage babysitters he'd used since arriving in Montana.

But he was full of unanswered questions. Why was she traveling if she didn't have a destination in mind? How did she pay for her expenses on the road if she was short of money to fix her car? Why did she say she needed a job? There was some sort of mystery here.

He didn't know this woman. He didn't know her past, her history, her experience. All he knew was she seemed to like children and her car had broken down. He would be foolish to put a stranger in charge of his young son. Lucas had been through enough in his short life without being put in the care of a woman with an intriguing past.

"*Ja*, I'll let you know," he replied in a neutral tone. He pointed ahead. "See that building? It's on the outskirts of town. It won't be long now."

"I hadn't realized I was this close. I'm surprised more vehicles didn't come by while I was waiting for help."

"You managed to get stranded on a seldom-used side road. There's a decent two-lane highway that passes by town, but for obvious reasons those of us driving buggies prefer to avoid the busier streets."

"Yes, I can see that." She fell silent a moment, clasping the child in her lap, looking around her with interested eyes as they came to the edge of town. "Seems like a nice place," she ventured.

"We like it. I've been here about a year now, and while it's sometimes awkward settling into a new place, the townspeople have been very kind to us."

Adam pulled the horse to a stop at an intersection and waited for traffic to pass before clucking the horse into a walk again. The main street of the town was lined with older retail businesses. He followed the street for a couple of blocks, then turned down a quiet side street and pointed. "See that building? That's the Millers' boardinghouse."

"Plain and simple," she said.

He chuckled. "*Ja*, that describes us very well, don't you think?"

He pulled the horse to a stop before a hitching post Matthew Miller—who normally ran the establishment—had installed last year on the edge of a parking area for the convenience of Amish customers. A sign by the street said "Miller's Lodging." He climbed out of the buggy and reached up to lift Lucas down. "Buster, *stay*," he commanded the dog.

Ruth climbed down from the other side. He fetched

her suitcase from the back of the buggy and led the way into the building's interior.

The small waiting area was deserted. It sported two lamps—an oil lamp and an electric one—along with some solid wood chairs and a colorful, braided rug. The windows had cream muslin fabric tied back to let in the late afternoon sunlight. The walls were wood panel, stained a lovely golden color.

Adam strode up to the desk and smartly tapped the bell. In a moment, Anna Miller came through a back doorway.

"Ah, *guder nammidaag*, Adam." The older woman, plump and cheerful, smiled.

"*Guder nammidaag*, Anna," he replied. "Where's Matthew? I thought he'd be watching the desk today."

"Matthew went back to Indiana for a few weeks to help our other son move out here. It will be so nice to have both our boys here in Montana."

"*Ja*, it will be. Anna, this is Ruth Wengerd. I found her stranded on the side of the road outside town. She needs a place to stay until she can get her car fixed."

"*Ja*, of course." Anna smiled at the younger woman. "I have a lovely room on the second floor with a nice big tree outside the window. Will that do?"

"Yes, of course." Adam saw her hesitate. "Um, I'm a bit low on funds. Can you please tell me the nightly rate?"

When Anna named the sum, he was glad to see Ruth's shoulders relax. He didn't know her financial situation, but at least she didn't appear destitute.

"Thank you," Ruth said. "That's fine. I'll be staying

at least one night, possibly more. It depends on how long it takes my car to get fixed."

"We do have weekly rates," said Anna, "so if your stay is more than a week, you'll get a discount. *Komm*, I'll show you where your room is."

Ruth turned to him. "Thank you for the rescue. As for you…" She squatted down and addressed Lucas. "Be a good boy for your daddy, okay? No running into roads." Smiling, she bopped him gently on the nose.

"Ja gut," replied the little boy. He smiled and abruptly threw his arms around the woman. She hugged him tight, and he saw her eyes close as she rocked the boy ever so slightly.

Adam's throat closed up. There was something about the gesture that reminded him of his wife. The tenderness with which she held her newborn son, the cruel cancer that took her away when Lucas was a year old… His wife had departed this earth knowing she would never see her son grow up.

He blinked and the vision disappeared. Instead he watched Ruth stand back up and touch Lucas on top of his head in a gesture of farewell.

"Thank you again," she told him. She seized her suitcase and followed Anna out of the room.

Adam took his son's hand and returned to the buggy, where the dog wagged his tail in greeting. "Stay," he reiterated again to the animal, then lifted Lucas into the buggy and unhitched the horse.

"I like her," Lucas pronounced as Adam swung the buggy toward home.

This was such an unusual observation that Adam

glanced at the boy. "She seems nice," he affirmed. "I hope she can get her car fixed."

The horse trotted easily out of town as Adam thought over the events of the last hour. She had offered her services as a nanny. What a pity she wouldn't be around long enough for that to come to pass, because that would solve so many problems for him.

The truth of the matter was, he could use a nanny. Badly. Lucas was an impulsive child, without a mother's guiding hand, and Adam had a business to run. He'd made do until now with a succession of babysitters, but so far no one had been steady and responsible enough to take Lucas under her wing.

What he needed, of course, was a wife. But in the meantime, a nanny might do.

Chapter Two

Ruth put her suitcase down on the bed and looked around. As Adam had warned, the room was very basic but squeaky clean, with cream-colored walls and hardwood floors, bare except for a small rug beside the bed. A bedside table held a lamp, a telephone and a clock. The room had two doors—one revealing a closet, the other leading to a small bathroom. The furniture was plain and made from pine—bed, dresser, bedside table and rocking chair. A colorful quilt covered the bed and a vase of flowers sat on the dresser. The evening sun streamed through a handsome oak tree outside the large window. The window was framed by pale green muslin curtains, through which she saw a glimpse of the pine forests and towering mountains that dominated the western side of the town.

The room reminded her, poignantly, of her childhood bedroom. "What a lovely room!"

Anna Miller smiled at the compliment. "Thank you. My husband and I own this building, but our son Matthew runs it. He's the one who furnished all the rooms."

"He has good taste." Compared to the dismal string of inexpensive motels she'd stayed in over the past two weeks, this little space shone like a gem. She touched the pretty quilt on the bed. "I haven't seen an Amish quilt since I was a kid."

"Oh, did you grow up in Amish country?" inquired Anna.

"Actually, I grew up Amish."

The older woman did a double take. "You did?"

"Yes. I was raised Amish until I was eleven years old and my parents left the church."

Anna's pale eyebrows elevated. "Ain't so? That sounds like quite a story."

"It is." The quilt brought back so many memories it was almost painful. From habit, she turned away from the rawness. "I suppose the first thing I should do is see if there's a mechanic in town. And a tow truck."

"There are, but they're probably closed by now except for emergencies." The older woman gestured toward the door. "There's a small restaurant about a block away that serves nice dinners. Or if you're in the mood for pizza, they'll deliver here."

The thought of holing up in this pretty room with a pizza and the book in her suitcase held a lot of appeal. "Actually, pizza sounds nice. I'll have to use the room phone, though. I left my own phone at a rest stop about a hundred miles away."

"Sounds like you've had a hard day."

"Yes. And thank you." Ruth smiled. "Or maybe I should say *danke*."

"Do you remember much of the language?"

"I didn't think I did until Adam started scolding his son after he almost ran into the road. I was surprised by how much I understood."

Anna nodded. "Adam has his hands full with that boy. He's a wonderful child, but he lacks a mother's guidance. Well, don't hesitate to have the pizza delivered downstairs. It won't be the first time they've delivered here."

Once Anna had departed, Ruth plopped down on the bed and stroked the quilt. Funny how it was the little things that sparked such strong memories. The clip-clop sound of the horse's hooves. The beauty of the hand-sewn coverlet.

For the first time in many years, Ruth let her mind wander back to the bewildering days when her parents had uprooted her from the Amish community where she'd been raised, and brought her to live in a new home in a new town. She had been severed from her former lifestyle as completely as if a knife had sliced her childhood away.

She closed her eyes and refused to dwell on the horror of the night her parents had died in a car accident, leaving her orphaned and bereft. She had done a decent job of blocking those memories and wasn't about to start dredging them up now.

In the meantime, she had some thinking to do. This time, as an adult, she was the one who had severed herself from her former life. She'd left behind her job and her apartment, cutting those ties because she was ashamed of her failures. This random, zigzag cross-country trip had helped her come to grips with the mess she'd made of her career, but it also meant she was something of a lost soul.

She wondered if she could find a job here in town. She needed to pay for her car repairs, yes, but she also liked the people she'd met so far. She was free as a bird. She could stay or leave as she liked. And at the moment…she seriously considered staying. She missed the ground beneath her feet, and Pierce seemed like a nice place.

The morning dawned bright and clear. Ruth wasted no time in using the Millers' phone to call a tow truck. The tow driver, driving a flatbed truck, swung by the boardinghouse to give her a ride to her vehicle.

"So you said it was a loud 'bang' followed by a lot of noisy clatter?" the driver clarified as he turned down the small side road heading out of town. He was bearded and tattooed and exuded a cheerful bonhomie.

"Yes. I didn't dare drive it any further."

"I'm not a great mechanic, but I can usually diagnose a problem, especially when it sounds serious like that," he said. "I recommend you bring it to Pierce Auto Repair. Their shop is on the other side of town. They're honest and up-front about what it might take to fix things."

"Thank you. I'm stuck here until it gets fixed." Her vehicle came into view as they rounded the bend. "There's my car," she added, pointing.

The truck driver slowed, pulled a U-turn across the road and parked in front of her car. He peered underneath and gave a low whistle. "Transfer case cracked," he remarked. "That must have made an awful lot of noise."

"Yes, it did." Ruth frowned. What was a transfer case and what happened when it cracked? "Is it fixable, do you think?" She clamped down on a sense of panic. It hadn't occurred to her that her car might not be drivable at all.

"I can't say without having it up on a lift. For now, let's get you into town. The mechanics at the auto shop can tell you more."

For the next fifteen minutes, Ruth stood by while the driver got her vehicle up onto his flatbed. She climbed into the cab of the truck and tried to respond politely to the man's chatter about life in the small town of Pierce. But her mind was buzzing.

What if her vehicle was effectively totaled? Thanks to the poor decisions she'd made in her job, she had very little money. She might have to lower her pride and go crawling back to her foster parents, begging them for a loan to buy another used car. Then what? Back to New York and her career?

Within a few minutes, the tow truck driver had pulled up in front of the auto repair shop. Ruth climbed out of the cab and watched as her car was lowered into the lot.

"Problems?" inquired a mechanic in grimy coveralls, wiping oily hands on a rag and offering her a smile.

"The tow truck driver said the transfer case is cracked, whatever that means."

The smile dropped from the man's face and he drew in a breath. "Ouch."

"That's what I was afraid of." Ruth sighed. "I don't

have a phone with me—I accidentally left it behind at a rest stop a long ways away—so for the moment I'm staying at Miller's Lodging in town. Do you know where that is?"

"Yes, of course. Nice people. That's fine, I'll look over the vehicle when I have a chance and leave a message with the Millers as soon as I can."

"Thank you." Blindly, Ruth turned and walked away. Her eyes filled with tears. She had a sinking feeling her car was a goner. Now what?

She walked toward the center of town. Pierce was less than a mile across, and the boardinghouse only about a fifteen-minute walk away.

Several businesses—including the local grocery store—had Help Wanted signs in their windows. Could she stay in town and earn her way toward another vehicle? It wasn't as if she had a destination in mind, anyway. And it was doubtful a small town like this would care about the debacle with her last job.

She paced along the sidewalk, thinking about her best course of action. What should she do? What should she do? Tears of self-pity welled in her eyes again.

A small commotion near the open door of a store called Yoder's Mercantile barely registered until a child came running out and smacked right into her legs. "Hi! Hi! Hi!"

It was little Lucas, his face a wreath of smiles as he hugged her skirt. Ruth couldn't help but smile back through her tears. She crouched down. "Hello! Nice to see you again."

Hot on the child's trail was Adam. "Lucas, *komm* here—" He stopped abruptly when he saw her.

Ruth rose. "Good morning."

"Good morning." He eyed her. "You look like you've had bad news."

"Let's just say it hasn't been a great morning." She scrubbed a hand over her face. "The tow truck driver brought my car to the mechanic a few minutes ago. He said the transfer case was cracked. I don't know what that means, but the mechanic didn't sound optimistic." She blinked back fresh tears. "It means I have no way out of here."

He rubbed his chin. "It's none of my business, of course, but how is it you had enough money for a cross-country trip but not enough to buy another used car if the need arises?"

Ruth didn't want to admit the atrocious state of her finances, or the embarrassing reason behind it. "Let's just say I'm on a limited budget."

"A credit card, perhaps?"

Her foster father had spent years lecturing on the dangers of credit cards. "I have a debit card, but I—I closed my account, so there's no money to back it up."

"Do you have family you can get hold of who can help you out?"

Again Ruth didn't want to admit her complex feelings toward her foster parents, or why she was reluctant to call them for aid. "I think I'd rather look for work here in town," she prevaricated. "Anna Miller said she could give me a decent weekly rate at the boardinghouse. And

I noticed a few Help Wanted signs around. I don't think I'll have any problem finding a job."

"And you said yesterday you didn't have a destination in mind, ain't so?"

"That's right." She smiled at his phraseology. She hadn't heard "ain't so?" since she was a kid—first from Anna Miller last night, now from Adam. "This doesn't seem like a bad place to get stranded for a month or two."

The man was silent a moment, looking at his son as the boy pressed against her leg. Then he spoke slowly. "Lucas hasn't stopped talking about you since we dropped you off at the Millers yesterday. You jokingly mentioned you might be interested in a nanny position. Is that something you'd consider?"

Ruth could hardly believe her ears. "A nanny? To this little one?" She touched the child's hair. "Yes! If you're interested, I'd be more than happy to work as a nanny. In fact, it would solve a huge problem for me."

"And me, too." The man smiled, his blue eyes grateful. "Maybe this was *Gott*'s timing."

"Maybe so." She hadn't thought about God in quite some time, but there was no question Adam's offer was timely.

Adam had to refrain from pumping his fist in triumph. A nanny! A dependable caregiver for Lucas! It was indeed the answer to prayer.

The succession of *youngies* he'd been hiring simply weren't reliable enough. He couldn't blame them— he remembered what it was like to be a *youngie*—but it did mean he couldn't really count on them when he needed to.

Just today, he had to take Lucas with him while presenting a quote to a prospective customer for his construction business. The child was impulsive, and Adam's attention was subdivided between presenting a professional front to the customer and keeping his son from going where he shouldn't.

In fact, he had stopped in Yoder's Mercantile to ask Mabel Yoder if she could recommend another teen to watch Lucas. But his son, it seemed, had made his own choice. Yes, maybe this was a *Gott* thing.

"How soon can you start?" He knew he sounded too eager, but he couldn't help it. Having Ruth working as a nanny solved so many problems.

Ruth gave a sniffly chuckle. "Right now, I suppose. I don't have anything else to do. But…but the rest of my things are still in my car. I'll have to transfer them to the boardinghouse. And I have to make arrangements with Mrs. Miller to stay longer."

"I tell you what. Let's spend today getting all the loose ends tied up. I can move things from your car to your room. You can make arrangements with Anna for a longer stay. Then I can bring you out to my place and show you around." He paused for a moment, unsure. "Are you okay caring for Lucas at my place?"

"Of course. Where else would I care for him?" Ruth squatted down level with the small child and smiled at the boy. In rough German she said, "It looks like I'll be taking care of you, Lucas. Is that okay?"

"Ja! Ja!" The child flung himself into her arms and hugged her.

Adam's throat closed at his son's obvious excitement. What was it about this stranger that his boy found so interesting? It was like he was pulled toward her like a magnet.

"That's fine, then. As for payment..." He offered a sum he hoped would suit.

Ruth rose, and he could see her making some mental calculations. "Yes, I would have enough to pay the Millers for my room," she mused out loud, "and put some money away, too. Accounting for food and other expenditures, I could save for another car..."

He was astounded at her ease with arithmetic. He continually struggled with numbers. But since she seemed satisfied with his offer, he leaned down to pick up Adam. He bopped the boy lightly on the nose. "Let's go help this nice lady move her things," he told the child, "and then you can show her around the farm. *Ja*?"

"Ja!" Lucas wiggled in his arms, his happiness obvious. "And Mindy! I can show her Mindy!"

"His kitten," he explained to Ruth. "I hope you don't mind cats."

"Not at all. I love animals."

And children, he thought. He had a fleeting impression about her—that she had a reservoir of affection that had been suppressed by circumstances in her past. Even as he felt it, he recognized it was an odd conclusion to draw.

It also underscored how little he knew about her, yet here he was entrusting his precious *boi* into her care.

He prayed he wasn't making a mistake, but he was at his wits' end. He couldn't balance a construction business and care for his son by himself.

"Well, let's get going, then," he said. "My horse is right there. We can go get your things from your car."

She climbed into the buggy with an ease that spoke to her childhood experience with them. He lifted Lucas up and she settled the child on her lap. Meanwhile he unhitched the horse, then swung up next to her. "Where am I going?"

She pointed down the main street. "Pierce Auto Repair, right on the edge of town."

"I know where it is. I've met the owner once or twice. Nice fellow." He set the horse at a walk as he directed the animal off the main street on to a secondary road, where there were fewer cars. Then he urged the horse to a trot.

"Ahhh…" Ruth gave a sigh.

He glanced at her. "What?"

"The sound of hooves on pavement. It just takes me back, that's all." A faint smile played on her face.

"You said you were raised in Pennsylvania?"

Her smile disappeared. "Yes. But after my parents were—were gone, I was raised in a foster family in central New York State." Her tone did not invite further questioning.

Adam was sorry he'd brought the subject up. There was some mystery here, something he didn't understand and felt he had no business probing. He smiled to himself. A woman with a mysterious past. It sounded like something out of a novel.

A few minutes later, he pulled his horse to a stop at the mechanic's.

"There's my car." Ruth pointed toward her vehicle.

He directed the horse and stopped in front of her car.

A man detached himself from under a vehicle on an elevated lift in the open garage. "Can I help you?"

"Good morning," Adam replied. "This lady brought her car here a little while ago."

The man's eyes shifted to Ruth. "Yes! I'm sorry, I haven't had a chance to look at it yet."

"I know," she replied. She lifted Lucas over and climbed down from the buggy. "But since it looks like I'll be in town for a while, I thought I'd get all my things out of the car."

"That's fine. Do you need a hand?" Adam noticed the man's eyes lingered on Ruth.

"No, thank you. I just found a job working as this little boy's nanny, so I'll be here for a while. I need to make some money to pay for car repairs. Or a new vehicle." She opened one of the car doors.

"I'll leave you to it, then," said the mechanic. "I should have a chance to look at your car by the end of the day."

With some amusement, Adam noticed the mechanic's eyes shift to him and thought he saw disappointment in his eyes. Did he think Adam was courting this woman? Either way, he sensed the man's interest withdraw from Ruth, who seemed oblivious to it all.

"Thank you." Ruth's voice was muffled as she extracted a box from the car.

"Come on, Lucas, let's help her get things from the

car," he told his son. He climbed down from the buggy and lifted the child out.

For the next few minutes they helped her to empty the vehicle. Ruth handed Lucas smaller items, which he solemnly carried to Adam to load into the buggy. There was an assortment of suitcases and boxes—some of which felt as if they contained books—and a guitar case. He wondered again why she felt it necessary to transport all these goods on what sounded like a rambling cross-country trip with no destination in mind, but he didn't ask.

"That's it," concluded Ruth. "That seems like a lot of stuff."

"We'll help you carry it to your room at the Millers'," offered Adam.

"Am I keeping you from your work?" she inquired, as she got into the buggy and reached for Lucas.

"Actually, this little one is," he said, handing up his son. "That's why it's worth my time to help you settle in."

"What is it you do?" she asked.

Adam picked up the reins and clucked to the horse. "Construction. I came here to Montana with the promise of a job building log cabins. I enjoyed the work, but since the company is located out of town, some of the jobs were taking too long to travel to, and I had Lucas to care for. There seems to be enough demand locally that I decided to start my own business. Right now I'm wrapped up in bids and proposals and plans, but finding reliable care for Lucas is what's keeping me from throwing myself into my work."

Like before, he noticed a fractional tightening of her

arms around Lucas, who seemed content to sit on her lap. The gesture warmed him. If *Gott* had indeed sent this woman to help him in his time of need, it seemed that tiny movement showed him a woman with a love for children.

Within a few minutes, he pulled up before the boardinghouse. *"Komm,"* he said. "I'll help you move in, then I'll take you to our house and show you around."

Chapter Three

In what seemed to be a pattern, Ruth held Lucas in her lap as Adam directed the horse and buggy out of town. Rapidly, the buildings dropped behind them and the road turned to gravel. She found herself surrounded by fields of cattle as well as what looked like harvested wheat. "No suburban sprawl," she observed.

"Not enough people in Pierce for that," he agreed. "Look ahead. Do you see that kind of half-enclosed valley?"

She followed his pointing finger. "Yes. From this distance it looks very pretty, very picturesque."

"It used to be a huge ranch," he told her. "Several years ago it went on the market, and the church bought it, then started divvying out parcels to anyone who wanted to settle out here. Land prices in Indiana and Ohio—and Pennsylvania, for that matter—are skyrocketing, so many younger church members who wanted a farm of their own jumped at the chance to get affordable land."

"Are you involved in building homes for these church members?"

"Quite often, *ja*. But many of the bids I'm entertaining are those of *Englischers* who are settling in the Pierce area. Log cabins are surprisingly popular in this part of Montana, and those of us in the church are learning why. Quite a number of church members like them. I learned a lot working for the company I just left, and have connections with a local mill that does their own logging. I don't do the actual assembly. I design and create kit homes. Right now I have three contracts to build cabins before winter, and it's pressing on me to get them done. I have my subcontractors lined up, but this little guy—" he reached over and tousled his son's hair "—was keeping me closer to home than I needed to be. That's why I think *Gott* had His hand in stranding you here. I sure could use the help."

Ruth felt the warmth of the child snuggled against her. The boy was quiet and she wondered if he was falling asleep. "I can't say I was too pleased with God when my car broke down," she admitted, "but I must say this works out for both of us."

"You're to consider my house your home," Adam continued. "I have it set up as a tiny farm—a couple cows, some chickens, a garden and orchard, that kind of thing. Lucas can show you around since he knows it like the back of his hand."

"He's not in school yet?"

"*Nee*, he'll go next year."

"Is there an Amish school?"

"Sort of. A lot of families homeschool their *kinder*,

but there's talk about opening our own school." The horse took a bend in the road, and Adam pointed again. "Look. You can just see my place now."

Ruth made out a smallish one-story log cabin surrounded by a generous fenced lawn and guarded by coniferous trees and rustling aspens, some of which were just starting to sport a yellow leaf or two. A barn and several smaller outbuildings came into view as they progressed along the road.

"Did you build this yourself?" she asked.

"*Ja*. Lucas and I stayed with some friends for the first few months after we came to Montana while I built this during my free time. We moved in when it was still unfinished…"

"And I hammered!" piped up Lucas.

Ruth chuckled. "So you helped your *dat* build the cabin?"

"*Ja*. It was fun."

"I think you'll have an apprentice as he grows older," she commented to Adam.

She saw a gleam of pride in his eyes. "He does seem to love everything associated with tools," he affirmed. "He has a miniature toolbelt and set of tools he loves to use."

As the trees parted, Ruth noticed a fenced construction site with a half-built log home only about a quarter mile from his house. "Is someone building right next to you?" she asked, surprised. "Considering how widely spaced apart all the farms seem to be, that's strange."

"No, actually, that's my log yard," he explained. "That's where we pre-construct the log homes. One of my subcontractors is an independent logger, so he hauls logs from a nearby mill. We build the cabins onsite, then disassemble them. Another contractor reassembles them at the customer's homesite. That way we work out any issues ahead of time, and the customer can make any changes before we finalize the design."

"I've never heard of such a thing."

"Actually, it's very common with the log home industry. It's like a giant toy set. *Ja*, Lucas?"

"Ja!" The boy wiggled in Ruth's lap.

Adam chuckled. "He's fascinated by the log yard. I have it fenced off, but he's wildly curious about it. Obviously it's too dangerous a place for a small child, though I take him with me when the other men aren't working so he can explore. But it's nice to be working so close to home most of the time. Unless I'm on a construction site, it means I can have lunch with Lucas."

He turned off the main gravel road and took a long driveway that sloped uphill a bit, over which cedars and red fir trees dappled the sunlight. Ruth breathed deep of the fresh air. "I've never been to Montana before," she remarked. "When I drove through the eastern half of the state, I was disappointed by how flat and treeless it was. But the western half is beautiful. All these secret river valleys and mountains and pine trees."

"And log cabins," added Adam as he emerged from the trees into the sunlit area around the house. He pulled up to the porch of the home on a semicircular driveway. "I'll unhitch the horse for the time being. I figure it will take an hour or so to show you around, then I'll run you back to town."

"Speaking of which, how will I get here each morning, since my car isn't working?"

"I don't mind picking you up."

"Thank you." To Ruth, his offer underscored how desperate he was for childcare for his son.

The yellow Lab bounced in excitement inside a fenced yard. "You've already met Buster," said Adam. "Fair warning, he'll lick you to death."

"That's okay, I like dogs."

The cabin was new enough that its logs still gleamed with a golden glow. Two rocking chairs and a small table were on the porch. Lucas scrambled ahead, climbing the broad porch steps with the alacrity of a monkey while Ruth followed. *"Komm!"* he exclaimed. "I'll show you my room!"

"Lucas, don't rush her," called Adam as he started unhitching the horse.

Ruth chuckled at the boy's enthusiasm. She followed him through the house, catching a blurred glimpse of living room and kitchen, until she arrived at his bedroom. Lucas leaped onto the unmade bed and started jumping up and down. "This is my room!"

"Your *dat* probably doesn't want you jumping on the bed," she said. Lucas impulsively launched into her arms, and she was hard-pressed not to stagger and fall at his sudden weight.

She laughed. "You're going to be a handful, I can see that. Show me your favorite toy."

He ducked out of her arms. "This," he said, darting over toward the window and plucking an item from a table.

It was a miniaturized leather tool belt with a hammer, pouches for nails, a wrench, two screwdrivers, pliers, and a small tape measure. She examined it, trying not to show her amusement. "This is wonderful," she told him. "I'm sure you're a big help for your *dat*."

"*Ja*. I want to be a carpenter, too."

"That's my boy," said Adam from the doorway.

Lucas tugged at her skirt. "What do I call you?" he asked.

The sudden question stumped her for a moment. *Miss Wengerd* seemed too formal. *Ruth* seemed too casual. "How about Miss Ruth?" she compromised.

"*Ja*, Miss Ruth. *Komm* and see the chickens!" He rushed out of the room.

But Adam caught the boy. "Hold on, *liebling*," he said. "Miss Ruth needs to see the rest of the house first. We'll show her the chickens in a few minutes." He quirked a look at her. "He's got a bit of an impulse control problem, as you can see. He's all go go go, and then he crashes during naps and at night."

She chuckled. "I was always told I had an impulse control problem, too. I think Lucas and I will get along very well."

"*Ja*." He rubbed his beardless chin. "Well, let me show you around."

For the next several minutes, he toured her through the cabin. It was comfortable but sparsely furnished as befitting a bachelor home for two males. The kitchen, kitted out with rustic wood cabinets and counters, had a wood cookstove as well as a modern propane range, with a large, plain oak table and four chairs. An old-fashioned icebox stood in lieu of a refrigerator. The walls were painted a pea green that offset the rustic wood beautifully. Off the kitchen was a large pantry, with plenty of shelves but very little by way of the jars of home-canned food Ruth remembered from her childhood. She touched one of the few jars of tomatoes. "Do you do your own canning?" she asked.

"*Nein*, I tend to survive on the generosity of neighbors. I have a garden like everyone else, but it seems I'm always too busy to keep it up or harvest things as I should. There are some neighbor ladies who help out with it."

The living room held a battered assortment of homemade and secondhand furniture over a braided rug, with oil lamps bracketed to the walls. The floor was scattered with toys and children's books, and books spilled out of two large bookcases built along the walls under the windows. The outer wall was logs, and the inner walls were painted a cheerful cream color. But over every surface, Ruth noticed a fine sheen of dust.

"I have an office over here," offered Adam. She followed him across the living room as he entered what turned out to be a small room with a large window. A cluttered desk, chair, oil lamp and bookcase were crammed inside. "This is where I do my bids and proposals."

"I see." The small room somehow had a chaotic energy to it—or was she imagining things?

Lucas tugged at his father's legs. "Chickens now?"

Adam chuckled. "*Ja*, chickens now," he agreed.

"*Komm!*" Lucas darted into the kitchen and through a back door.

"He's full of energy," observed Ruth as she crossed the living room toward the kitchen. "Does he ever tire you out…"

She broke off as she heard a thump and a wail. Adam darted ahead of her and out the back door. Ruth followed, her heart pounding.

Lucas had tripped going down the steps off a small back porch, and lay at the bottom with a skinned elbow. Adam pulled him to his feet and swung the child into his arms. "There, there," he crooned, patting the boy on the back as Lucas wept big tears. "You fell down again, *ja*? It's *oll recht*…"

Lucas sniffed into his father's shoulder for a moment or two. Then, unexpectedly, he leaned away and reached out his arms for her.

Adam felt a moment's confusion when his son stretched out his arms for Ruth, but without a word he transferred the child into her arms. Lucas clung to the woman and buried his face in her shoulder. Adam felt mixed emotions. For the last few years, since his wife passed away, it had been just him and Lucas. His son had never really warmed to any of the babysitters they'd had. What was it about this stranger that the boy found so appealing?

Ruth swayed the child back and forth for a few moments, then gave him a little bounce. "Do I have the impression your *dat* has warned you about those steps before?" she asked in a teasing voice.

Lucas sniffled and pulled his face out of her shoulder. *"Ja,"* he admitted.

"And how many times have you fallen down them?"

Adam could see the little gears whirling in the boy's head. "A lot," he said after a moment.

"Ja, a lot," Adam agreed. "I keep telling him one of these days he's going to break an arm."

"But for now, it's just a skinned elbow." Ruth lifted the boy up and made an exaggerated kissing, smacking noise on the reddened skin. "There! All better?"

The child giggled. *"Ja."*

"Now, where are those chickens you wanted to show me?"

"Over there!" He immediately wiggled out of Ruth's arms and would have gone barreling away had Adam not caught him on the shoulder.

"Slowly, little man," he warned him. "Miss Ruth doesn't have your speed."

Lucas moved in the direction of the chicken coop at a sedate trot, and Adam fell in with Ruth across the back lawn. "He loves the chickens," he explained.

"So I gathered." Ruth's gaze roamed about. "So, what other animals do you keep?"

"Just a couple of milk cows." He pointed toward an adjacent pasture where two Jerseys grazed with calves at their sides. "An older lady who lives nearby takes a lot of my extra milk and makes cheese for me."

"Look, my favorite chicken!" cried Lucas.

Adam chuckled as his son, inside the chicken yard, held aloft a compliant hen. "For all his hyperactivity, he's very *gut* with animals," he told Ruth. "He's quite gentle with his kitten and the chickens."

"It seems that way." Ruth unlatched the coop gate

and stepped inside. "What's your chicken's name?" she asked him.

"Cluck-Cluck." Lucas stroked the bird's head and lightly scratched her under her beak. "She lays brown eggs."

"She's very pretty."

"I help *Dat* feed the chickens and pick up eggs."

"You're a good helper, then."

"Ja." The child grinned up at her, an adoring look on his face.

Adam blinked. For an eerie moment, he saw his son looking up at Ruth with the same expression he used to have as he looked at his mother. But that was impossible. Bethany had died before Lucas could walk, much less gaze at her adoringly. He shook his head and the eeriness faded away. But it left a lingering unease. He wondered if somehow Lucas wasn't already looking at Ruth as a mother figure.

"Well." He cleared his throat, trying to dispel the mental moment of disquiet. "Let me show you around the cow barn and the garden, then I'll run you home."

With Lucas bounding ahead full of importance to show Ruth the cows, he reflected on his son's reaction to the new nanny. Should he be worried? It wasn't that Ruth didn't seem like a fine woman. But she, like every other woman in Lucas's short life, was transient. He worried the boy might become attached to someone who would leave town as soon as her car was fixed or she could afford to buy another vehicle.

But there was nothing he could do about it. He needed help caring for Lucas during an especially busy time with his business, and Ruth was the solution to that problem. He would worry about the outcome later.

He walked through the open barn door into the shadowy interior. Hay bales were stacked to the ceiling through most of the barn, with a wide path between them toward the back, where a series of stalls were situated.

"By the way, Lucas is strictly forbidden from climbing the hay bales," he told her. "He understands that, but it's still a temptation for a small and energetic boy. Please don't let him up there."

Ruth tilted her head up at the mountain of bales. "I can see why he's tempted," she admitted. "But yes, I'll remember that."

Lucas was already ahead, jumping up and down in front of a milking stall. "This is where we milk! And I help!"

Ruth quirked a glance at Adam. "Does he really?"

"Actually, *ja*. He's never too young to learn to milk. And it takes time to build up the hand strength. It's one of our morning chores. Right, *sohn*?" He tousled the boy's hair.

"*Ja*. And I'm teaching my kitten to drink milk when I squirt it at her. Look, there she is." Lucas darted over and scooped up a sleepy orange-and-white, half-grown feline from a low bale of hay. "This is Mindy."

"She is sweet." Ruth took the cat in her arms and cuddled her. Then she looked at Adam. "It's nice to be on a farm again. I've spent far too many years in the city. Seeing cows and chickens—it brings back such memories."

Adam found himself curious about her past, but now was not the time to ask personal questions. He'd probably find out more later on. Instead he said, "Lucas, do you want to show her the cows?"

"Ja!" The boy darted out a back door of the barn, and Adam followed Ruth into the sunshine and the confines of a fenced-in corral.

An open gate at the other end of the corral led into a pasture, now mostly yellow after the summer's dryness. Two placid fawn-colored cows lay in the shade of several majestic firs, chewing their cud, with two half-grown calves grazing nearby.

"Lucas, stay in the corral," ordered Adam, as the boy seemed inclined to bolt toward the animals. "The cows are perfectly gentle," he told Ruth, "and Lucas is used to being around them. But he's kind of in show-off mode right now, and I don't want him doing anything rash."

She laughed. "Yes, he's all enthusiasm. He'll calm down after a couple days with me, I'm sure. Are the cows off-limits, too?"

"No, not at all. The only thing off-limits is climbing the hay bales, and the log yard. Lucas is used to shadowing me in all my chores, since of course I can't leave him alone. I've drilled him over and over on how to be safe around the place, and for the most part he understands."

"He seems like a bright boy, just a little impulsive. It's something I can sympathize with." She crinkled her face, as if afflicted by a painful memory.

To cover her obvious embarrassment, he said, "Let me show you the garden. Lucas! Do you want to show Miss Ruth your vegetable plot?"

"Ja!" The child bolted back toward the barn.

Adam chuckled as he and Ruth followed Lucas through the barn and out the front. Lucas made a dash toward the left, where a tall fence protected the vegetables from deer.

"He rushes here, he rushes there. Does he ever slow down?" Ruth asked.

"Ja, sure, when he's asleep. And then he sleeps *hard*." He shot her a look. "Do you think he'll be too much for you?"

"I doubt it, but I'll let you know."

She seemed unfazed by the boy's energy, which Adam took as a good sign.

He opened the latch to the garden gate—which was too high for Lucas to reach—and stood back to let Ruth and his son pass through.

Ruth stood at the edge and gave a low whistle. "Looks like you grow just about everything you need."

"Close to it," he agreed. "But that's normal for gardens, ain't so? If you grew up Amish, you must remember that."

"Yes, I remember. I also remember it was a lot of work to preserve everything before winter."

He rubbed his chin. "Yes, it's work," he agreed. "The woman who makes my cheese also does a lot of my preserving in exchange for keeping some for herself. My… my wife used to do much of that before Lucas was born, but it's been a long time." He hated that his voice still caught when mentioning his deceased wife. He wondered if the pain would ever go away.

Ruth glanced at him but didn't probe. Instead she

said, "I might turn my hand to some preserving if I have time. It's something I've always been interested in."

"You're welcome to do whatever you want. As I said before, consider my home to be your home while caring for my son."

"Look at the pumpkins, Miss Ruth!" crowed Lucas, straddling a generous gourd that showed the faintest flush of orange on its green rind.

"I see." Ruth waded out through the rows toward the child. "What's your favorite vegetable?"

"Corn!" The child jumped off the pumpkin and ran toward the stand of rustling corn. "Can I have some for dinner? Can I? Can I?"

"That's up to your *dat*. I won't be here for dinner. But come here and tell me if it's ripe."

With some amusement, Adam watched Ruth peel back the top of an ear and invite Lucas to examine the tip. She seemed to remember more about gardening than she realized.

Lucas touched the tip. "I—I think so…"

"Yes, it looks ripe to me. Tell you what, we can have corn for lunch tomorrow when I'll be here all day, okay?"

"Okay."

"You seem to be *gut* with kids," he observed as she straightened up.

"I like kids, sure. After my parents died, I was raised by a foster family. I spent a lot of time caring for the younger foster children they were raising. But I also figure if my job is taking care of Lucas, then the best thing to do is involve him in everything. Besides, it will help him expend all that pent-up energy."

"He seems quite taken with you." His gaze rested on the child, who skipped between rows of tomatoes and beans.

"I think this job will work out just fine. I'm more grateful than I can say to have it."

"Same here." He glanced at the sun. "But I'd better run you back to town. I have work to do before dark."

He called Lucas back to his side and left the garden. Skirting the side of the house, he started re-hitching the horse while Ruth lifted Lucas into the buggy.

"What time can I expect you tomorrow?" inquired Ruth as he started on the road back to town.

"Will seven o'clock be too early? That way we'll be back here by seven thirty or so, and I can get to work by eight o'clock."

"Seven o'clock is fine. I'm an early riser anyway."

In the bustling town, Adam turned down a side street to avoid most of the car traffic. He pulled up beside the Millers' boardinghouse. "Tomorrow morning at seven, then," he told her.

"I'll be right here, waiting." She gave Lucas a smacking kiss on the cheek. "We'll have a fun day tomorrow, won't we?"

"Ja!" The boy wiggled with excitement as she handed him over and climbed down from the buggy.

He clucked to the horse as Lucas fell into an atypical silence as they headed out of town. He glanced at his son. "Are you okay?"

"Ja," the boy replied solemnly. Then, with a cheeky grin, he pronounced, "I like Miss Ruth."

"I do too, *sohn*," he replied. "What a wonderful thing

that she'll be able to keep an eye on you while I'm working." He paused. "Don't misbehave, okay? No disappearing like you did with Bella. Or with Sarah. Or with Mrs. Yoder."

"*Nee*, I won't disappear," Lucas declared earnestly. "Not if it's Miss Ruth taking care of me."

Adam couldn't help but smile at his boy's childish hero worship. He only hoped Ruth wouldn't be overwhelmed by his small son's impulsive behavior.

Chapter Four

Adam was prompt, Ruth learned the next morning. She positioned herself on the sidewalk in front of the boardinghouse at five minutes before seven o'clock. It was a crisp fall day, and the neighborhood's mature maples and oaks were just barely starting to turn color. Five minutes later, Adam pulled up in the buggy.

"Miss Ruth! Miss Ruth!" Lucas practically squealed with excitement.

Ruth chuckled. "Good morning to you both. Here, little man, get on your *dat*'s lap for a moment while I get in." Lucas obligingly scooted over until she had climbed aboard, then immediately settled on her lap.

"And how are you this morning?" she asked Adam as he directed the horse out of town.

"Fine, *danke*. Glad and relieved you're available to watch this little monkey. I have a full day of work ahead of me." He gave her a smile that could only be described as brilliant, and his blue eyes crinkled. "In fact, it's the first time in a long time I've been able to *plan* a full day of work without worry or concern. I didn't realize how much my attention was subdivided toward Lucas's care until I didn't have to obsess over it anymore."

Ruth smiled, feeling the quivering excitement of the child in her lap. "Give me an idea of your daily schedule," she said. "Has Lucas had breakfast yet?"

"Just some toast and butter. He might be hungry later on, before lunchtime."

"And when does he nap?"

"He's outgrown his morning naps, but he usually crashes in the afternoon for at least ninety minutes."

She nodded. After caring for a series of younger foster siblings during her teen years, such a schedule sounded typical. "And you," she said. "Didn't you say you normally come home for lunch?"

"*Ja*, if I'm not working off-site."

"Then I'll make lunch for everyone."

Adam frowned. "I'm not paying you to cook for me," he said. "I'm paying you to look after Lucas. Don't feel you have to do anything extra."

"I can feed two people or I can feed three people. No big deal." She thought for a moment. "I have a few recipes in my repertoire, and hopefully you have some cookbooks in the kitchen."

"I do, *ja*. As I said, you're to consider my home your home."

"Thank you. Or maybe I should say *danke*. It wouldn't hurt for me to start remembering the language of my childhood."

As Adam pulled up in front of the house, Buster the dog bounded out to greet them and Lucas broke into more chatter about what he hoped to do while under her care. Ruth smiled. She'd missed children during her years as a working professional. Lucas was just one child, but he had the energy of two. Fortunately, she had a lot of experience under her belt when it came to kids.

"I'll put the horse away, then I'm going right over to the log yard," said Adam, handing down Lucas after she climbed out of the buggy. "I'm right nearby if there's an emergency."

"We'll have a fun day, won't we, Lucas?" Ruth took the boy's hand and led him into the house as the excited dog pranced around them.

She started by having Lucas take her on a more leisurely tour of the farm, encouraging him to show her his favorite things. She discovered his "fort" tucked under a bush. She watched as he searched for eggs. She helped him pick some ripe tomatoes and greens for a lunchtime salad.

Best of all, he was tired enough before lunch to snuggle into a porch rocker and listen to some stories. Feeling the warm little body in her arms as she turned the pages of the book, Ruth realized she had put thoughts of motherhood on hold for many years. In fact, she had not seriously considered having children at all. Now here was this darling boy…

"Do you think grilled cheese sandwiches and a salad is enough for your *dat*?" she asked him. "What else might he like?"

Lucas thought a moment. "He likes cookies," he offered.

"I won't have time to make any for lunch, but maybe

you can help me make some for dinner. What kind of cookies?"

"Oatmeal raisin!" Lucas wiggled in his seat.

Ruth had a sneaking suspicion those were Lucas's favorites, not Adam's, but it didn't matter. "Then we'll make some this afternoon," she told him.

She heard a knock at the front door. Opening it, she saw a matronly older woman in Amish dress and *kapp*. The woman looked surprised to see Ruth. "Good morning," she faltered. "Is Adam in?"

"He's out working in the log yard," replied Ruth. "My name is Ruth Wengerd. Adam just hired me to be Lucas's nanny for the next couple of months."

"*Ach*, it's nice to meet you." The woman held out a hand to shake. "I'm Nell Peachey. I make cheese for Adam from the milk he gives me. I came to pick up today's milk." She gestured behind her, where a pull cart with large wheels rested.

"I'm afraid I don't know how much he gives you…" Ruth hesitated.

"I can find my way around, if you don't mind." Nell smiled.

"Of course. Please come in." Ruth stepped back.

Nell headed toward the kitchen where Lucas sat at the table with milk and crackers. "*Guder mariye*, young man," she said. "Are you being a *gut* boy today?"

Ruth was able to follow the chatter as Nell and Lucas spoke in *Deutsch*. Feeling daring about her language skills, she said in the German dialect, "Lucas and I are having a good time."

Nell's head snapped around, shock plainly written

on her face. Speechless for a moment, she finally sputtered, "You speak *Deutsch*?"

"I was raised Amish," Ruth explained in English. "My parents left when I was a child, so it's been many years since I spoke the language. But the more I hear it, the more I remember."

"That's *gut*, then." Nell seemed satisfied. "It means you can feel more comfortable if you bring Lucas around to play with other children."

"Yes, you're right." Ruth smiled at the older woman. She sensed an ally.

"Now, all the milk I'll need should be in here." Nell opened the door to the old-fashioned icebox with an air of familiarity. "*Ja*, here it is." She removed several half gallon jars of milk, the cream thick at the surface. "Please tell Adam I'll bring him the green cheese tomorrow. He knows to store it in his root cellar until it's ripe."

"I'll tell him." Ruth helped carry jars and followed Nell, her own arms loaded, as she walked outside. The older woman placed all the jars in a crate, seized the wagon handle and walked away.

Ruth slowly closed the door. All the women she'd grown up with had made cheese. It was one of the better ways to use up surplus milk. Nell's bustling, slightly bossy air was achingly familiar.

There were so many housewifely skills she had not learned, such as cheese making and food preservation. She might remember how to milk a cow, even though it had been so long. But could she learn or relearn some of those skills while she was here? Would people like Nell be willing to teach her?

Yet, what was the point? She was here just long enough to earn money to either repair her car, or buy another. Then what? Another month or two of wandering? Or returning to New York to a job she realized she didn't miss? What did the future hold in store for her?

For the moment, she had an eager boy to care for. She walked back into the kitchen and found Lucas's chair empty.

For a minute she stared at the chair dumbly. "Lucas?"

No answer. Suppressing a moment of panic, she walked to the open back door and looked out into the fenced yard. "Lucas?" It would be just her luck to lose the boy the first day on the job. No answer.

"Lucas!" She practically shouted his name. Her heart clutched in dread as she remembered Adam's warning about the boy climbing that mountain of hay bales in the barn. Could he …? She tensed and got ready to dash toward the barn.

A muffled voice stopped her. *"Ja?"* It sounded like it was coming from below the house.

She walked down the back porch steps and saw Buster the dog wagging his tail in front of a doghouse. "Lucas, are you in the doghouse?"

"Ja, I'm a dog. *Komm* and see."

She crouched down and saw the boy, a smear of dirt on his cheek, grinning at her. She could hardly yell at him for engaging in such a harmless activity, and she willed her beating heart to slow down. Obviously, this was a child who must be watched every second of the day.

"It's time to make grilled cheese sandwiches for lunch," she told him. "I came to see if you want to help me."

"Ja!" He scrambled out of the doghouse and got licked in the face by Buster. "I'm hungry!"

"Even though you just had some crackers? Well, come inside. I'll slice the cheese and then you can help me assemble the sandwiches. I'm guessing your *dat* will want two. Let's go get you washed up." She dropped a relieved kiss on top his head.

He clambered ahead of her up the porch steps and dashed to the kitchen sink. She smiled despite herself. The kid had nonstop energy. She had her work cut out for her with this one.

Adam straddled a log and dragged a tool across the wood to remove the bark. He realized it was one of the first times in a long time he could utterly focus on his work without having to worry about Lucas or who would watch him the next day or the next week.

His instincts told him his son was in good hands. He thanked *Gott* once again for sending Ruth his way.

At lunchtime, he left his crew eating in the shade of a tree and walked the quarter mile home, curious how the morning had gone. He stepped into the kitchen to see Ruth and Lucas sitting at the table, with grilled cheese sandwiches and salad in bowls in front of them.

"Gut'n owed," he said.

"Dat!" Lucas squirmed in the booster seat on his chair.

He dropped a kiss on his son's head and quirked a

glance at Ruth. "You still look like you're in one piece," he observed with a smile. "That's *gut*."

"We had a fine morning," she replied. "And we're going to make cookies this afternoon. Lucas said you like oatmeal raisin."

"*Ja*, we both do." He moved to the sink to wash up, conscious that he had a sheen of sawdust over his clothes.

"I wasn't sure what time you would be home, so I let Lucas eat," she told him as he sat down.

"That's fine." He waved a hand. "My schedule is never exact, so don't ever feel you have to hold a meal for me." He dropped into a chair, closed his eyes for a silent blessing, then reached for the salad. "So tell me about your morning. What have you done?"

"We picked tomatoes from the garden," supplied Lucas. "And I got eggs."

"And Nell Peachey came by for milk," added Ruth. "She seemed to know what she was doing, so she just came in and got the jars she needed and said she'd bring you some cheese tomorrow which you're supposed to store in your root cellar, wherever that is."

He nodded. "Sorry, I forgot to show you the root cellar. Lucas can show you where it is. Nell is my nearest neighbor and a very nice woman."

"I remember my *mamm* making cheese when I was very young," she said with a touch of wistfulness in her voice. "I found myself wishing I could learn. Maybe Nell could show me sometime."

"I'm sure she'd be happy to, but…" His voice trailed off. He thought it would be rude to point out the obvious—that she wouldn't be here long enough.

She seemed to snatch his thought out of the air. "You're right, what's the point? It's not like I could make cheese when I return to New York."

He took a bite of his sandwich. "Meanwhile, if you're ever up for a walk, there's a family about a half mile away named Eva and Daniel Hostetler. They have three *kinder*, the middle one a boy about Lucas's age. I'm sure Eva would love to meet you and have Lucas and her son play together sometime."

"I'll remember that." She took a bite of her sandwich and chewed thoughtfully. "It's such a different pace out here, at least from what I've seen so far. No hustle and bustle, no horns honking or traffic. Just neighbors being neighborly."

"Do you miss the city?"

Her face took on a faraway look for a moment. "No. At least, not yet. It's hard to tell. For the last few weeks, I've just been wandering wherever the spirit took me, so I haven't really been in the city in quite a while."

He sensed again a sort of mystery about her, something disquieting in her past she seemed eager to avoid. He'd never met anyone "wandering" wherever the spirit took them, and he wondered if that wasn't code for avoiding a painful incident or leaving someone behind.

But ultimately, it was none of his business. So far she seemed to be doing a good job watching his son. That was all he should care about.

In fact, Lucas seemed eager to chatter about the morning. Adam observed how his son interacted with Ruth. He had long ago learned to pick up subtle cues about the quality of the caregiver by how his child behaved. From what he could see, Lucas adored Ruth. He was still in the eager, show-off phase of their acquaintanceship, but Ruth seemed unfazed and up to the task of handling his son's considerable energy.

Yes, this was certainly *Gott*'s doing, to send him a caregiver when he needed it most. He said a silent prayer of thanks, finished his grilled cheese sandwich and wiped his lips. "I'm heading back to work now. I'll be back around five o'clock to drive you into town." He rose and deposited his plate in the sink. "*Danke* for lunch. It was delicious."

"You're welcome." She remained seated next to Lucas. He dropped a kiss on his son's head and walked back to the log yard.

"Got a call while you were out," reported Peter, his foreman. The man handed Adam a scribbled paper. "Someone is interested in another quote for a cabin on the other side of Pierce."

Adam scanned the man's messy handwriting. "*Danke*, Peter. I'll call them shortly." Though he would prefer not to use a telephone at all, in accordance with Amish lifestyle, the church recognized the need for many businesses to be able to communicate and had allowed him to install one in the little office building in the log yard.

He also tamped down a sense of dread. Consultations and bids and quotes were a part of running a business, but it was the part he liked least. He wondered if he should hire someone more at ease with numbers than he was. He understood every element of construction and truly enjoyed working with logs, but when it came to putting numbers on paper, he struggled.

He placed a phone call to the interested party, a family named Johnson, who had just moved to the area and purchased a plot of land outside Pierce. They were interested in building a log cabin. Adam smiled. He'd met this kind before—urban transplants eager to embrace the whole Montana experience, and what could be better than a rural lifestyle in a log cabin outside a tiny town?

Glancing at a clock on the office wall, he told them he would stop by that afternoon, around three thirty. He would look over their land and recommend building spots. Also, he'd bring a notebook with some of their standardized floor plans.

After he hung up the phone, he went to relay the conversation with his foreman. "They sound fairly convinced they want a log home," he concluded.

Peter gave a low whistle. "Could we get another done before winter? That would mean four to complete before the snow flies."

"I think we can manage this last one, but that's it. Anything else will have to wait until spring." Adam removed his hat and ran a hand through his hair. "I had no idea we'd have this many orders so soon. I hope we didn't bite off more than we can chew."

"A nice problem to have, but still a problem," agreed Peter.

Adam gathered the materials he would need to take with him while meeting the prospective new clients. He had told Ruth he'd be finished by five o'clock to drive her back to town, but now he wondered if he'd be home by then. Walking over a jobsite and discussing financing with clients was not a cut-and-dried thing. He puzzled over the logistics for the needs of the nanny as well as his son.

Unless…

"I'll be back in about fifteen minutes," he told his foreman.

He headed home and walked into the kitchen to a scene of happy chaos.

"Dat!" yelled Lucas, his mouth sticky with cookie dough and flour all over the table. "I'm helping!"

"So it seems." Adam smiled at his son, then addressed Ruth. "I have to go to the other side of town to meet with some prospective clients at three thirty," he explained. "I said I'd be home by five to take you back to town, but I don't know if I'll be finished by then. Would it be possible to take you and Lucas with me and drop you off in town? You could play with him in the park or walk around. Then I can pick him up on my way home."

"Of course. That will be fun, won't it, Lucas?"

"Ja." The child bounced in his chair and spilled some flour on the floor.

"You might want to put him down for a nap a bit early, then." Adam smiled with relief. *"Danke,* Ruth. Okay, *sohn,* you keep being a *gut* boy for Miss Ruth. I'll see you in a couple hours."

He walked back to the log yard, much more at ease. Bless Ruth and her flexibility. He wondered if he could convince her to stay until the winter, when conditions shut down most of his business for a few months.

At least, that's what he told himself. But deep down, he found himself hoping Ruth could just stay.

Chapter Five

Ruth read Lucas a story and then put him down for a nap. She fully anticipated the child would fight sleep, but to her surprise he made no protest. When she checked on him a few minutes later, he had crashed. She remembered what Adam said—that his son played hard and then slept hard.

With an hour to herself, Ruth tidied up the mess they'd made in the kitchen. Noticing the fine sheen of dust on every surface in the rest of the house, she wiped away the evidence of bachelor neglect. She stacked Lucas's toys in a shallow wooden crate in the living room put there for that purpose, then damp-mopped the dusty floors. The whole tidy-up took less than half an hour, and Lucas was nowhere near finished with his nap.

She decided to anticipate dinner and poked around the kitchen and pantry, trying to think of what to make. The pantry was disorganized but held a wide variety of items. She found jars of home-canned chicken, pork, green beans, carrots, corn and other vegetables mixed randomly with jars of applesauce, peaches, pears, blue-berries and plums. Jars of spices were lined up on shallow shelves behind the door. She found tubs of lard and buckets labeled "cornmeal" and "sugar." She itched to make the small room more organized—vegetables and savory items on one side, fruits and preserves on the other—but of course it wasn't her house.

She picked up a jar of canned chicken and considered it thoughtfully. She remembered, from her childhood, a favorite recipe of her mother's—chicken potpie. She had often made the dish in her foster home, where her overwhelmed foster mother recruited anyone and everyone to help with the cooking and feeding of so many mouths. Could she recreate that meal?

In the kitchen she found several cookbooks, and within minutes found a recipe for a version of the dish. Raiding the pantry again for a mixture of vegetables for the filling, and lard for the crust, she assembled everything else she needed and started following the recipe.

It took longer than she thought, but the finished product was lovely. She stood back, a foolish grin on her face as she looked at her handiwork. Why would she feel more pride in making a humble chicken potpie than she did engaging in all the high-level financial transactions in her last job? Her cheeks grew hot as she recalled the humiliation, the mistakes, the failures she'd left behind in New York City.

But that was all behind her now. Somehow she found herself here in this tiny mountain town in this vast state, taking care of a rambunctious little boy…and liked the prospect.

She glanced at the clock: two thirty. Adam would be by in half an hour. She cleaned up the kitchen, put the unbaked pie in the ice box, and turned to see Lucas standing behind her, rubbing sleep out of his eyes.

"You're awake. How did you sleep?" Ruth bent to lift the child into her arms. He put his arms around her neck and rested his head on her shoulder, still too tired to say anything. Ruth's heart melted at the instinctive gesture. She made her way into the living room and sank into a rocking chair, rocking the boy as he emerged from the fog of sleep.

Within five minutes, he stirred. "Hungry," he mumbled.

"We made cookies this afternoon, remember?" she said.

The child brightened. "*Ja.* Cookies!" He clambered off her lap and dashed into the kitchen.

Ruth chuckled. She was learning Lucas had no middle ground. He was either sleepy or fully active.

The boy was just finishing his snack when Adam walked through the door carrying a large leather case. He seemed distracted. "I'm going to go hitch up the horse," he told her, stopping to tousle Lucas's hair. "Can you be ready to leave in five minutes?"

"Yes, we'll be ready." Ruth made sure the boy had his shoes and socks on and his hands were washed. She and Lucas were ready by the time Adam pulled the buggy around.

As they headed toward town with Lucas on her lap, Adam glanced at her. "*Danke* again for being this flexible. Where would you like me to drop you off?"

"I don't know the town well. Is there a park with a playground?"

"*Ja*, a very nice one. It's not far from the Yoders' store. Why don't you let Lucas play in the park until about five o'clock, and then meet me at the store?"

"That sounds good. Do you like swings, Lucas? Or seesaws?"

The boy seemed confused by the English terms, so she translated to *Deutsch*, and he brightened. "*Ja*, swings."

Ten minutes later, Adam pulled the horse to a stop in front of a small but beautiful leafy park, with maple and oak trees just starting to turn color and a few children on the playground.

"*Danke* again, Ruth. I'll meet you in the Yoders' store." He touched his hat and took off, the horse's hooves clip-clopping on the pavement.

She watched him go. For just a moment she was part of a family, with a child at her side and a husband on his way to work. For just a moment she belonged somewhere, rather than a small part of an ever-changing foster dynamic with substitute parents who were distracted by many cares.

Then she shook her head, took Lucas's hand and headed for the playground.

Before they had reached the sanded area, Lucas shouted "Jacob!" and made a dash for another boy dressed in Amish garb. The children grabbed hands, chattering, then headed for the slides.

"Careful, Jacob!" called a young matron, a pretty woman with a *kapp* and black apron.

Intrigued, Ruth made her way to where the woman sat

with a small baby sleeping on her shoulder. "Your son?" she inquired, jerking her head toward the other boy.

"Ja," the woman replied with a smile. "And that's Lucas, ain't so? Are you watching him?"

Ruth sat down uninvited and held out a hand to shake. "Yes. I'm Ruth Wengerd. Adam Chupp just hired me to be his nanny for a while. This is my first day on the job."

"Nice to meet you." The infant sighed, and the woman shifted the baby's position. "I'm Eva Hostetler."

"Oh, you're the neighbor Adam mentioned," exclaimed Ruth. "He said I might want to meet you in case your son wanted to play with Lucas."

"Ja, the boys often play together." Eva examined Ruth a moment. "Do you live here in Pierce? How did Adam come to hire you to watch Lucas?"

Ruth gave a rueful chuckle. "Actually, I was traveling from New York City and my car broke down outside of town. Adam rescued me and helped me get a room at the Millers' boardinghouse. I needed a job to pay for car repairs, and one thing led to another. Now I'm Lucas's nanny until I can earn enough to either pay the mechanic, or buy another used car."

She saw Eva's forehead wrinkle with unasked questions, and was grateful when the other woman refrained from delving into what was still painful. Instead, all she said was, *"Gut.* Adam could use the help. Lucas needs a firm hand. He's an endearing child, but lacks a mother's steady guidance."

"I'm used to looking after children," confided Ruth, watching as her charge tumbled about with his friend.

"I grew up Amish, though my parents left the church when I was very young. I was very surprised to see an Amish community this far west."

Eva startled. "You grew up… I see." She was clearly fighting the urge to ask more.

"I think that's why I never cared for fashionable clothes," Ruth mused, plucking at her skirt. "I never quite fit in in New York, where I worked. Maybe that's why I like it here so far."

Eve smiled a lovely smile. "It certainly seems *Gott*'s hand was involved somehow."

"That's what Adam said, and I'm inclined to believe him." Ruth found herself drawn to the young mother. It would be nice to have a friend while she remained in town. "I left behind a career I didn't like," she confessed. "My job kind of…blew up on me. I was taking a cross-country trip, with no destination in mind. That's why I don't mind staying here for a bit and working as Lucas's nanny. It's better than what I left behind."

She hadn't meant for emotion to creep into her voice, but that was precisely what happened. But Eva seemed like a woman of rare discretion. She simply shifted her baby to another position and nodded. "Then *welkom*," she said simply.

Ruth blinked back tears at the sincerity in the other woman's voice. To distract from what she was feeling, she asked, "How old is your baby?"

"She's two months old. Her name is Grace."

"May I see?"

"Of course." Eva held out the baby.

Ruth took the infant in her arms. The baby was sleeping, looking rosy and content. Ruth hadn't held an infant in a long time—not since her foster parents had taken in twin babies shortly before she left for college many years ago. A thrill went through her at the feeling of holding a baby again.

"She's beautiful," Ruth breathed.

Eva glanced at her watch now that her arms were momentarily free. "I'll need to go shortly," she commented. "I'm meeting my husband at Yoder's Mercantile at five o'clock."

"I'm meeting Adam there, too," replied Ruth. "He said it was easier to bring Lucas to town and pick him up on the way back through. He said to meet him at Yoder's. Is that an Amish-run store?"

"Haven't you been to Yoder's?" asked Eva in surprise.

"No. I just saw it from outside yesterday morning."

Eva smiled. "It's a wonderful place, and kind of a natural gathering spot for our church members as well as the *Englischers* in town. They have a small play area for children conveniently placed next to a little tea shop. *Komm*, let me buy you a cup of tea until the men show up."

Ruth smiled and handed the baby back. "Thank you. Or rather, *danke*. I should start remembering to use the language I was born to."

Eva called to her son and Ruth called to Lucas. The boys ran up, panting and dirty. She grinned at the little boy entrusted to her care. Already she was starting to feel at home in the community. It was a welcoming feeling.

Adam shook hands with his new clients, the Johnsons, zipped up his leather case and climbed into the buggy—an act which in itself seemed to enchant the middle-aged couple, who had never seen an Amish buggy before. But as the horse trotted away, he smiled to himself. They would be *gut* customers, he could tell. Reasonable, open to suggestion, and interested in a modest-sized home, not the log McMansions that he personally didn't like but which, unfortunately, were too often associated with Montana. He'd told the couple he would provide plans and an estimate within the next week.

His shoulders slumped at the thought of crunching the numbers, however. He could build and construct, hammer and saw practically in his sleep. But when it came to estimates or bids or even taxes, he would actually lay awake at night worrying. He had a feeling he would have to hire someone in the near future to handle that facet of his company.

Still, because the couple were interested in a small-ish one-story cabin, he was certain he and his crew could get it done before the snows came. Only if Ruth could stay until his work season was over for the winter, that is.

Whatever mystery might lie in her past, he thanked *Gott* he had stumbled upon her broken-down car when he did. Was it only two days ago? It seemed longer.

He directed the horse through town and parked in front of Yoder's Mercantile, where Abe Yoder had thoughtfully provided hitching posts for his fellow church members. He recognized Daniel Hostetler's rig as he climbed down to tie up the horse.

The store was busy, as always. He glanced around,

hoping Ruth would be here, and was pleased to see her sitting in the small café with Eva Hostetler. Nearby, in the low, walled-off children's area, Lucas played with Jacob, Eva's son.

He strode over. "*Guder nammidaag*, Eva," he said.

The young mother looked up. "*Guder nammidaag*, Adam," she replied. "Guess who I met in the park while Jacob was playing?"

"I can see." He seized the back of another chair and moved it to the table where the two women had mugs of tea in front of them.

"How did your meeting go?" she asked him.

"Very well. They agreed to use my company. I have to provide them with plans and an estimate by next week."

"That's good, then. Lucas was a good boy, especially when he saw his friend in the park." She gestured toward the two boys.

Daniel Hostetler, Eva's husband, came over from where he had been conferring with some other men. "*Guder nammidaag*, Adam. How's business?"

Adam chatted for a few minutes with the other man as Eva and Ruth fetched the children from the play area. Adam was amused to see smudges of dirt on Lucas's face and clothes. His rough-and-tumble son could rarely go to bed without a bath.

"We must go," said Eva, swaying her infant in her arms. "Our daughter is visiting at Mary Lapp's place, and I'm sure everyone wants to get home for dinner. Ruth, would you like to bring Lucas over to play with Jacob the day after tomorrow?"

"Yes! Thank you, I'd like that." Adam saw Ruth's face light up with pleasure. He was glad she'd found a friend.

After the Hostetlers had departed, he gestured toward her mug of tea. "Take your time finishing it. I don't mind sitting for a few minutes." He settled back into the chair with a sigh. "Looks like you found a friend."

"Yes. What a nice woman." She pulled Lucas onto her lap. The boy seemed content to sit quietly, enclosed in her arms. "Lucas made a beeline for Jacob at the park, so it was kind of a natural thing for Eva and me to chat while the boys played. She has a lovely new baby."

"*Ja*, Eva's a *gut* mother." He changed the subject. "How did your first full day on the job go taking care of my *boi*?" He reached over to tousle his son's hair.

"He was great." Ruth gave the boy a gentle bounce in her lap. "While he took his nap, I made a chicken potpie. It isn't cooked yet, but it's in your ice box. You can have that for dinner."

His eyebrows shot up. "That was kind of you, but don't feel you have to make us dinner. You're doing enough, keeping an eye on Lucas."

She shrugged. "I had nothing else to do while he was napping. Besides, it was rather nice to rediscover some of my kitchen skills."

He shook his head, smiling. "Well, are you up to continuing the job after today's trial?"

"Of course." As before, he saw her arms tighten fractionally around the child. "He's a good boy, and we had fun. Didn't we, Lucas?"

"*Ja!* We made cookies."

"Then all is right." He chuckled, then turned serious. "This new bid looks like it will pan out, and—well, it gives us four homes to complete before winter. It's a heavy schedule, but I think we can manage it, as long as Lucas has *gut* care." He paused, suddenly nervous. "So, ah, how long can I convince you to stay as his nanny? Could you manage it until we're finished with these projects?"

She hesitated, and Adam felt a prickle of sweat as he considered what would happen if she refused. He would be back on the eternal treadmill of finding temporary care for his son.

"How long would that be?" she asked. "When does winter shut you down?"

"Around mid-November. We never know when the first snowfall comes, of course, but we like to get as much completed before the end of November as possible."

"So that's about two months away," she said thoughtfully. He noticed a faraway look in her eyes, as if mentally figuring her schedule. Then she shrugged with, he thought, a trace of defiance. "Yes, I'll stay. There isn't much for me back east at the moment."

He'd never stopped to consider before, but he wondered if her unusual cross-country trip had been the result of a love gone sour. That might explain her apparent reluctance to return, though he did wonder what she had expected to do for income during her trip. Again he detected some sort of mystery about her, something she evaded discussing.

At the moment she seemed satisfied to care for his son. Lucas seemed thrilled with her. And Adam was more grateful than he could say for the arrangement.

"Danke," he told her gravely. "This solves many issues for me. When I moved out here to Montana, I didn't realize how much I depended on the support system I had back in Indiana for Lucas. Here, I lack that support. Having consistent care for him during my busiest season is a huge relief."

"Maybe you should remarry," she suggested.

Remarrying was something he'd considered—and dismissed—before. The reasons were always the same. *"Ja,* I've thought about it," he admitted. "And the bishop has brought it up a time or two, but it seems rather heartless to marry simply to find someone to care for Lucas, ain't so? Besides, there aren't a lot of single women my age in our church. They're all too young for an old bachelor like me with an active boy. Another reason I sometimes wonder if I did the right thing, moving out here."

She sipped the last of her tea. "I think I'll say goodbye and head back to the boardinghouse."

"Can I drive you there?" He rose and took Lucas into his arms as she transferred the child.

"No, thank you, it's just a short distance away. This town is so compact it's no trouble to walk places. I got used to walking everywhere in New York. Besides, I'm anxious to see if the mechanic has figured out whether my car is fixable."

"Okay. *Danke* again. Shall I pick you up again tomorrow morning at seven o'clock?"

"That will be fine." She dropped a kiss on Lucas's head. "See you tomorrow. Okay, sweetheart?"

"Ja."

Lucas waved as she headed out the door. Adam hitched the boy higher on his hip. "Ready to go home?"

"Ja. I'm hungry, *Dat."*

"Miss Ruth mentioned she made a chicken potpie. Doesn't that sound *gut*? *Komm*, little man, let's go feed the animals while the pie cooks."

Outside, he lifted Lucas into the buggy, then unhitched the horse, swung into the driver's seat and headed out of town.

"I like Miss Ruth," Lucas remarked thoughtfully.

"I do, too. I'm glad your first day with her went well."

The child gave a cheeky grin. "And it took her a long time to find me in Buster's doghouse."

Adam frowned. "What did I tell you about running away?"

"I didn't run away, *Dat.* I was just hiding in the doghouse, right by the back door."

"Was it a game she was playing with you? Did Miss Ruth know you were hiding?"

"Nee..."

"Then it was running away." He gave the child a tap on the shoulder. "It's scary when you do that, *sohn.* I want you to promise you won't hide again, not unless it's part of a game."

"Oll recht, Dat." Lucas's voice was earnest. "I won't."

Adam sighed. Though the pain was softer, there were times he missed his deceased wife with a deep ache. This was one of those times. Bethany would have known how to handle Lucas's mischievous behavior.

He hoped that eventually, Ruth would know how to handle his rambunctious *sohn*, too.

Chapter Six

Her car wasn't fixable.

Hanging up the phone with the mechanic on a Thursday afternoon, Ruth stared at a bare spot on the wall at the boardinghouse. The transfer case was indeed cracked, the mechanic told her. It would cost far more to fix it than the value of the vehicle.

Oddly, the news upset her less than she'd thought it would. In the one week she'd been in town, she had gotten into a rhythm with both her job and her living situation. She was being careful with her spending. At this rate, she would be able to afford another second-hand vehicle in two months, about the time Adam said his busy season would be over. And for the time being, she didn't mind living at the boardinghouse. Most of her waking hours were spent with Lucas anyway.

"The only thing I miss about having a car is being able to drive to Adam's," Ruth remarked to her landlady, relating her conversation with the mechanic. "It's terribly inconvenient for him to hitch up the buggy, pick me up early, drive me to his place, unhitch the horse, then finally make it to work—all because his place is too far away to walk and I have no car."

"I have a bicycle," suggested Anna Miller. "It belongs to my son, but since he's away at the moment I'm sure he won't mind if you use it."

"What a good idea!" Ruth brightened. "It wouldn't take me much longer to get to Adam's by bicycle than it would by buggy."

Ruth followed Anna's plump form to a shed behind the boardinghouse. The older woman pulled out the bike with a ragged basket in front, and gave the seat a cursory dusting. "It's an older model," she apologized, "but I believe the brakes work without a problem."

"May I try it out?" Ruth took the handlebars from her.

"Of course." Anna stepped out of the way.

Fortunately, the bike was a model with a lower top tube, so she could straddle it in a skirt without issue. She rode up and down the side street, testing the brakes, changing gears. The bicycle was fine.

"If you're sure your son won't mind, I will gladly use this," she said to Anna after she returned. "The basket will be handy if I need to bring anything with me. I don't have any way to contact Adam before he picks me up tomorrow, but I'll see if I can fit it in the buggy when he comes by in the morning. That way he won't have to drive me home in the evening."

She was feeling pleased with herself the following morning as she waited for Adam on the sidewalk before the boardinghouse, with the bicycle parked beside her. When the familiar clip-clop of the horse's hooves sounded, she looked forward to telling him his schedule would be easier. She waved to Lucas as the child bounced with excitement at seeing her.

Adam pulled the horse to a stop and returned her grin. Pointing at the bike, he asked, "Is that yours?"

"It's Anna Miller's. She said I could use it. I figure it won't take any longer to ride a bicycle to and from your place than it takes to fetch me in the buggy. If we can squeeze it the back of the buggy, I'll take it to your place and you won't have to take me back here this evening. I would have let you know in advance, but there was no way to reach you."

"Ja, gut." He tucked the reins in the holder and climbed out of the buggy.

The bicycle stuck out the back at an awkward angle, but Adam wedged it in so it wouldn't fall out. Ruth climbed into the buggy and Lucas dropped onto her lap. "And how's my little man today?" she asked in *Deutsch.* She had been trying to use the language more and more, and it was getting easier.

"Gut! Dat made me pancakes for breakfast."

"Yum. And what would you like for lunch?"

She listened to Lucas's chatter as Adam took up the reins and directed the horse out of town and down the gravel road leading to the Amish enclave, which included Adam's cabin.

She glanced sideways at him. "I finally heard from the mechanic yesterday evening," she ventured. "He said my car wasn't fixable. Or rather, it would cost more to fix it than the car is worth. The news isn't surprising, to be honest."

"Does this upset you?" He glanced her way.

"Less than I thought it would. I'm fine working for you, and I'll have enough saved up to get another second-hand vehicle by the time your busy season is over."

He nodded. He must be relieved, she thought. But he abruptly changed subjects by commenting, "I wonder, though. Isn't your family worried about you?"

"I have no family," she said quietly. "Remember?"

"But you have foster parents, *ja*?"

"My foster parents are wonderful, but I was simply one of a long line of kids they've taken in. When I was younger, I called it the conveyer belt. Older kids would leave and make their way in the world. Younger kids would come in. Some were there for only a little while, days or weeks. Others were there for several years, until they aged out of the system. I never grew close to anyone, because what was the point?"

He winced. "I'm sorry. I didn't realize it was that bad."

"It wasn't," she said hastily. "That is, I was one of the lucky ones. There were many children demanding their attention, and they did their best to give each kid what they needed. But it was easy to get lost in the chaos. Sometimes there were as many as fifteen children they were taking care of. My foster parents worked very hard with the older kids to make sure they could earn a living once they left home. They had a very high success rate. But I don't think they're particularly worried about me or even notice I'm not in New York anymore."

It seemed strange to talk about her tumultuous adolescence. It was not something she felt comfortable discussing.

"I wondered why you were so *gut* with Lucas," he commented after a moment. "Were you put in charge of handling the younger children as they came into the family?"

"Many times, yes. I seem to have a natural gift for taking care of little ones, and it was a way to help out the people who came to my rescue when my parents were killed. I didn't mind."

"You're a *gut* woman, Ruth."

The quiet remark stunned her momentarily. It seemed to come from a deeper well than simple gratitude for taking care of Lucas. Ruth sat still, trying to untangle and decipher any deeper meaning.

Adam pulled up to the barn behind the cabin, greeted as always by Buster's enthusiastic welcome. "I must say, if this bicycle works out for you, it will ease up my schedule," he admitted as he extracted the contraption from the buggy.

"I'll let you know tomorrow morning." After watching him store the bike in the barn, she took Lucas's hand. "Come along, little man, let's go plan our day."

She spent the morning following the routine she had set up over the last week—mostly keeping Lucas as physically active as possible—but inside she kept gnawing, like a dog with a bone, at what Adam had said. *You're a good woman, Ruth.* Why had that simple statement shaken her so much?

She didn't want to admit how much his words warmed her. They were more rewarding than the wages she got from him, and far more than the paycheck she had earned—and squandered—in the job she'd left behind in New York.

"Let's play hide-and-seek!" suggested Lucas before lunch as they spilled out of the house into the warm fall sunshine.

Ruth had an uneasy memory of his disappearance into the doghouse the week before. "How about tag?" she suggested instead. She crouched down and pretended to stalk him. "I'm gonna get you!"

Lucas fled, giggling, while she chased him. When Buster ran toward the front yard, barking and wagging his tail, the child diverted his course and headed for the gate. "Jacob!"

Ruth straightened up and waved to Eva Hostetler walking by, the baby in her arms and two other children circling around her. Her son, Jacob, headed over to the fence to chatter with Lucas.

Eva followed and spoke to Ruth over the fence. "Would you like to come for lunch in a little while?" she inquired. "Maybe half an hour, after I put this little one down for a nap?"

"Danke!" Ruth grinned. Eva had been very patient through Ruth's groping attempts to recapture her *Deutsch*. "Are you sure it won't be any trouble?"

"I'm sure, *ja*. I have another friend coming, who has a daughter Millie's age." Eva gestured toward her six-year-old, who smiled shyly. "So it will be a nice lunch party and the children can play afterward."

"Can I bring anything?"

"Just yourself."

"We'll be there." Ruth felt a flush of happiness at

being accepted. Eva's gentle friendship over the last week had been a lovely thing to experience. The young mother was calm and patient with her children, and warmhearted enough to draw in a stranger—even an *Englisch* stranger. Almost against her will, it seemed Ruth was being more and more accepted by this community.

At lunchtime, Adam walked into an empty house. Buster bounced around, but seemed lost without Lucas there. On the kitchen table was a note from Ruth explaining the invitation from Eva Hostetler, and informing him that two sandwiches had been left in the ice box for his midday meal.

He put the note down with a smile. It was nice that Ruth was getting invitations from others and that Lucas had a chance to expel some of his energy by playing with Jacob. And how thoughtful of Ruth to keep his lunch ready.

He sat at the table, said a quick blessing and bit into the meal. It was just the kind of sandwich he liked. Had Ruth been taking notes about his preferences?

Buster lay down under the table and issued a sigh of what sounded like frustration. He felt like echoing the dog's feelings. Without Lucas—and Ruth—the house seemed unnaturally quiet. A clocked ticked over the kitchen door. Birds sang through open windows. Chickens cackled in the coop. But it seemed empty without his son.

And Ruth…

He hated to admit it, but he missed her presence, too.

He took another bite of his sandwich and wondered if his interest in the nanny was morphing into something else. Ruth was not of his faith. That put her strictly off-limits.

But that didn't keep him from taking notice of her. His eyes roamed around the kitchen, noting some of the little things that indicated her presence. The dishes neatly washed. A platter with a display of colorful leaves in which she had placed the salt-and-pepper shakers.

Restless, he walked around the house. Lucas's bed was neatly made and the toys in the living room were confined to the shallow crate he'd made to hold his son's playthings—except for some wooden train tracks that snaked around a couple of chairs. It almost seemed the room was less dusty, too. He grimaced, wondering what Ruth must have thought of his easy bachelor ways.

In short, after just one week, Adam didn't know how he'd ever managed Lucas without Ruth. For that matter, he wondered how he'd ever managed his *own* life without Ruth in it. The woman was a marvel of efficiency She was patient and kind to Lucas. And subtly, without fanfare, she was taking care of him—Adam—as well He hadn't enjoyed such domestic tranquility since his wife passed away.

Smiling, he patted the dog and walked back toward the log yard. He knew Lucas was thriving under Ruth's care. He just hoped that when it came time for Ruth to leave, his son wouldn't be too shattered.

Or himself, either.

When the day's work was finished, Adam walked to

his house. He could smell something delicious cooking before he even got inside the yard fence.

"*Dat!*" cried Lucas, running for him.

Adam caught his son up in his arms and spun him around once. "I heard you played with Jacob today. Is that right?"

"*Ja!* And Thomas, too."

"And did Miss Ruth get to visit with the *mamms*?"

"*Ja*. They drank tea or something." Lucas wiggled out of his arms. "Come see what Miss Ruth is making for dinner! I helped!"

He chuckled as he watched the child dash up the back porch steps and into the house. The screen door slammed behind him.

More sedately, Adam also climbed the steps and entered the kitchen. He saw Ruth and froze.

She had evidently found one of Bethany's old aprons and wore it while taking something out of the oven. For one excruciating moment, he saw his wife in front of him. Then Ruth straightened up, turned and smiled. "Hello."

He blinked away the pain and the memory, but was left shaken by the coincidence. Ruth looked nothing like Bethany. She wore modest clothes, but not Amish garb. Why should he suddenly see the wrong woman?

"*Guder nammidaag.*" He turned automatically to wash his hands at the sink. "Whatever you made smells delicious."

"It's a recipe Eva gave me. She called it 'dump and go' casserole. I knew you had all the ingredients, so I decided to give it a try. Lucas helped me after he woke up from his nap this afternoon." She winked. "That way he's sure to like it."

Adam chuckled. He looked to where the table was neatly set for two. "You aren't eating with us?" he asked, surprised.

She seemed just as surprised. "No, why? I just thought I'd head home."

"Where do you normally eat dinner?"

"At a restaurant around the corner from the boardinghouse."

"You worked so hard to make us a nice meal. Please eat with us." He gestured toward the table. "It will save you the cost of a restaurant meal."

She stared at him for a moment, then nodded. "Okay. Thank you." She laid another place setting and put the casserole on the table.

It was just like a family.

Together, they shared a silent prayer, then dug into the casserole. "This is *gut*," he remarked on his first bite. "What else happened at Eva's this morning?"

"I met another woman named Mary. Eva offered to show me how to can vegetables if I'm interested. And Nell offered to show me how to make cheese." He saw a wistful look cross her face. "My mother used to can and make cheese. I hadn't thought about those things in years."

He decided to probe delicately. "Do you know why your parents left the Amish?"

"No. It was something they never wanted to discuss." She poked at her food. "And later, of course, they were gone and I couldn't ask them."

"You have no siblings?"

"No. I don't know the details, but I think my parents weren't able to have any more children. It was strange being the only child in a community of large families, though of course after we left the church I learned lots of people only have one or two kids."

"And your foster parents. How old were you when they took you in?"

"Twelve. I stayed with them six years, until I was eighteen and went to college. They're wonderful, my foster parents."

"Yet you don't think they're worried about you staying here in Montana for any length of time?"

"Not really." She took a bite, then spoke with her mouth full. "I stay in touch, of course, but I haven't been home in quite some time." She swallowed. "Their goal, as they put it, was to launch me out into the world as a successful adult. Once I was out of the house, their attention naturally turned to the children they were still caring for at home."

"So you went to college. What did you study?"

"Finance and business." He saw her face start to shutter, but he pressed on.

"And after college? What did you do?"

"I went to work on Wall Street." Her expression was definitely closed now. "It wasn't—I soon realized that it wasn't my cup of tea. Some stuff happened and I left my job. End of story."

End of story? Not likely. Adam burned to ask her more questions, but she clearly wasn't in the mood to answer them. Nor did he have any right to press. It was none of his business. But that element of mystery around her deepened.

"I should go." Ruth glanced at the clock, scraped up the last of the casserole from her plate, and rose to put her dishes in the sink. "I think the bicycle will work out well, at least until the weather turns bad." She dropped a kiss on the top of Lucas's head. "I'll see you both in the morning."

While she didn't exactly run out the door, Adam had the distinct impression she was fleeing his questions. He felt a little guilty for pressing so far, but he found he wanted to know everything about her—including what sent her on this mysterious cross-country trip.

"I like having Miss Ruth here," observed Lucas, talking with his mouth full.

"Me, too, *sohn*. Me, too." The house somehow seemed dull and listless without her. He watched as she pedaled away, a small trail of dust on the gravel road following in her wake. "How fortunate we found her on the road when we did, eh?"

"*Ja.*" Lucas swung his legs and kicked his heels against the chair legs. "I wish she was my *mamm*."

What could he say to that? Lucas, in his childish innocence, had no idea of the wider ramifications of such an innocent statement.

But in some of Adam's quieter moments, he, too, wondered what it would be like if Ruth was Lucas's *mamm*.

But courting her was impossible. Not only was she

not Amish, but she was only passing through, and had a mysterious past to boot. Not exactly the type of solid, dependable woman a man should look for in a second wife.

He hoped Lucas would not be too disappointed that such a wish could never come true.

He hoped he wouldn't be too disappointed when it came time for Ruth to move on, either. He was almost afraid to see her in any light except as a nanny.

Chapter Seven

Sunday morning dawned. Ruth stood at the window in her room at the boardinghouse, looking down at the quiet street. What was it about the Sabbath that made a small town look so quiet and thoughtful? From her vantage point, she could see a number of church steeples in the distance. She even heard bells pealing from one of the unseen houses of worship.

The few people walking down the sidewalk were dressed up and looked solemn and purposeful. A few cars drove along the road, doubtless with a church as a destination.

It was a different feeling here in this small town of Pierce—so different than the constant bustle of New York City, where Sunday was just another day for most people. But in this tiny remote town, the citizens seemed to hearken back to an earlier time, a time when church attendance was simply expected. It seemed almost like a time capsule from decades before— small-town America on a Sunday morning.

The boardinghouse was quieter than usual. Not just because she was the only guest at the moment, but because Anna and Eli Miller were away at their own church services. Ruth remembered how long Amish services could run—three hours at least, with a generous potluck lunch afterward.

A memory came back—a hymn she used to love singing as a child. She hummed it now, trying to recall the words, but the lyrics eluded her.

Restless, she turned away from the view and picked up a book. She hadn't been to church in a long, long time. Not since her parents were alive. Her foster family never attended church, simply because the logistics of transporting so many children—many of whom had special needs—was too difficult. They never discouraged faith, but never encouraged it, either.

During her college years, and then after she graduated and began her career, somehow faith had been pushed into a distant corner of her mind, a memory that she pulled out now and then. Now she wondered if it was still alive and salvageable.

She didn't know. Could faith be salvaged? Could the church of her childhood still have meaning and purpose for her? Could she attend an Amish service and be welcomed?

She looked down at her clothing. She realized now why she had always preferred to wear skirts instead of jeans or slacks, and had no particular interest in fashion but preferred to stick with plain and unassuming garments: Amish women wore only dresses, and her own clothing choices as an adult unconsciously reflected her upbringing.

Ruth put her book down and reached for her guitar. A month ago she would have reached for her phone, using the tiny screen and constant connection to the wider world as a distraction. Now she didn't miss her phone at all. She liked feeling in control of her time again. She preferred the feel of the guitar strings under her fingers. The instrument had served as a stopgap for loneliness many times, especially while living in New York, when a social life was nearly impossible with her work schedule. Often she had dragged herself back to her apartment after midnight, forced herself to eat something healthy, then spent an hour unwinding with music.

She spent a few moments tuning the instrument, then started picking out a melody—the hymn she had tried to recapture earlier. It was slow going, but in the end she was satisfied. If only she could recall the words.

She sighed, rested the guitar back on its stand, and then did something she hadn't done in a long time: she picked up a copy of the Bible the Millers provided in every room of the boardinghouse. She opened the volume to the book of Matthew and started to read.

"But I want to see Miss Ruth." Lucas's voice held a distinct whine.

Adam suppressed a sigh and strove for patience. Lucas had been restless and fractious ever since Friday afternoon when Ruth had pedaled off on her bicycle, the week's work done. Now, just before the beginning of the church service, he hoped his hyperactive son would be able to handle the lengthy observance.

"You'll see her tomorrow," he remonstrated. "Lucas, do I need to remind you of the proper behavior on Sunday?"

The child quieted down but remained sulky. Adam filed into the large barn on the Stoltzfuses' property, newly cleaned for services, and took a seat on the men's side.

Lucas allowed himself to be held on Adam's lap during the singing of hymns. It had taken a long time to train the active child to adopt a quiet demeanor during services. He wondered if Bethany would have had an easier time of it.

He knew from his own experience as a young boy how difficult it was to sit still during church services. It took training to teach children respectful behavior. Lots and lots of training.

He permitted himself a small smile, remembering some boyish naughtiness of his own. He recalled the time he had smuggled a frog indoors, and the amphibian had escaped his grasp and caused some consternation on the women's side. That was why he was both strict and understanding when it came to Lucas's own difficulties and hyperactive tendencies.

But the child made it through the service without further problems. Released at last, Lucas dashed away to play with some other boys outside.

"Trouble?" inquired Anna Miller, a quirky smile on her face. "Lucas looked restless."

Adam chuckled. "Was it that obvious? *Ja*, he was

like a little monkey today. He kept saying he wanted to see Ruth. He's very taken with her."

"Ach, she seems like a *gut* woman. I'm glad she's working out as Lucas's nanny."

"Is she a *gut* tenant at the boardinghouse?" he asked, curious.

Anna nodded. "The best. She's quiet and neat. I hear her playing her guitar sometimes, but not loud enough to disturb anyone else. Not that there's anyone else at the boardinghouse right now," she chuckled.

"Dat?"

Adam looked down to see Lucas at his knee. *"Ja, sohn?"*

"Can we go see Miss Ruth today?" The child tugged on Adam's trousers.

Adam looked at Anna Miller in some exasperation. The older woman chuckled.

Adam squatted down at eye level with the boy. "Today is the Sabbath, Lucas. Miss Ruth deserves a day of rest like anyone else, don't you think?"

"Maybe we could go to the park?" persisted Lucas. With unusual insight, he added, "I can play and she can rest."

"There's that park in Pierce with a nice walking path along the creek," suggested Anna.

Adam raised his eyebrows. If he didn't know any better, he would think the older woman was matchmaking. He stood back up and lifted Lucas into his arms. "Okay, *sohn*. We'll go into town and see if Miss Ruth would like to take a walk in the park."

"Danke, Dat!"

* * *

Ruth heard Anna and Eli Miller's buggy return. Looking out her window, she saw the horse passing underneath before turning a corner to the stable and tiny paddock in the back, where the animal was kept.

Her restlessness had not decreased. Putting aside the Bible, she went downstairs to greet Anna. "How was the church service?"

"It was *gut*." Anna winked. "But there was a small boy who kept asking for you."

"Oh." She smiled. "He's a darling, that Lucas."

"Don't be surprised if you see him today. Thanks to Lucas's pestering, Adam said he might see if you're interested in going for a walk along the creek that runs through town."

Ruth felt her cheeks heat, and knew the blush was noticeable. She kept her voice steady. "That would be fine. I wouldn't mind seeing more of the area."

"Have you had lunch? If not, there's some chicken salad in the refrigerator."

"Thank you, I am a little hungry."

Anna, she knew, felt protective about her and had graciously given Ruth access to the kitchen. Often she invited Ruth to help herself to leftovers.

Anna's husband, Eli, done stabling the horse, came into the house and removed his hat. He yawned and stretched out his arms. "*Ach*, I think a nap is calling my name," he remarked.

"It's a *gut* day for it, *lieb*." Anna smiled at her husband, then nodded to Ruth. "As I said, help yourself to anything in the kitchen."

The couple disappeared to their quarters in back, where Ruth knew there was a caretaker's apartment. Ruth watched them go in some amusement. She liked seeing older people in a happy relationship. The Millers were the epitome of contentment, two doves sharing a nest. She vaguely remembered her parents had a similar level of serenity. Not for the first time, she wondered what had pulled them away from their Amish roots.

It was an old and unanswerable question. Before she could dwell on it too much, Ruth headed to the kitchen to raid the refrigerator as Anna had urged.

"I warn you, she might have other plans," Adam told Lucas as the horse trotted toward Pierce.

"But I just want to see her," Lucas whined.

"You'll see her tomorrow, regardless. But she might be up for a walk today. However, no nagging at her, *ja*? If she doesn't want to go, she doesn't want to go."

"Ja, Dat." Lucas stared out at the scenery. Adam could almost see the boy quivering with excitement—all over seeing a woman he'd seen all day, every day, for the last week.

He pulled the horse to a stop before the boarding-house and climbed out of the carriage to tie up the horse at the hitching post. "Best behavior," he warned Lucas, lifting the child down and taking his hand.

Adam walked into the lobby and saw Ruth immediately. She sat in one of the lobby seats, idly plucking the strings of her guitar. Lucas immediately broke off and dashed toward her. "Miss Ruth!"

"There's my little man!" Ruth put the instrument

aside and gave Lucas a hug, then looked up at Adam. "Anna said you might come by."

"*Ja*, Lucas wouldn't stop talking about you. I told him you deserve your day off, but…"

She waved a hand. "I was bored, to be honest."

He hated to admit how pleased he was by her interest. "Let me go unhitch the horse, then we can check out the park by the creek. Can Lucas stay here for a moment?"

"Of course. In fact, he can come with me to my room to put my guitar away and grab a sweater. Shall we go upstairs?" she asked the child, taking his hand.

"*Ja!*"

Adam wondered what her room looked like, but could hardly ask. Instead, he went outside to unhitch the horse and stable it for a couple hours with the Millers' horse.

By the time he was finished, Ruth and Lucas were waiting on the porch for him. *Just like a family*, he thought. A family going on a Sunday outing in the park.

"Is it far?" Ruth asked, falling in beside him as Lucas skipped at her side, holding her hand.

"*Nein*, just across the main street and a couple blocks down. Since this park by the creek isn't in the center of town, it doesn't get as many visitors as the park where you met Eva Hostetler. But it has swings and some sports fields, and after the park ends the walking path along the creek keeps going for a couple more miles."

"Sounds lovely. It also means we can let this little guy run around and burn off some energy."

"*Ja*, I confess that was part of the plan." He grinned at her. "He can be a high-maintenance child."

She locked eyes with him for a moment, then looked

away. "He's just being a boy," she said. "Nothing wrong with that."

They navigated through the town's streets. Traffic was quieter, but more people were walking about after church. Within five minutes they were at the edge of the park.

"Swings!" Lucas pulled his hand from Ruth's and darted toward the play area.

Adam gave a sigh of exasperation. "At least he can't get hit by a car here. He's so impulsive."

"I was much the same way when I was younger. Some say I still am." She kept her eyes on the boy, but her face wore a grim expression.

"Like the impulse to take off and drive cross-country?" he asked in a teasing voice.

She snapped her head around. "Yes, exactly so." Her grim expression was replaced by a smile.

He didn't want to get caught up in her pretty brown eyes. Instead he pointed. "The path starts over there, along the trees."

He called Lucas back, and the child ran ahead of them, exploring.

"I've never seen such a compact town," she remarked as the municipal buildings and homes fell behind and grassy fields stretched ahead, bisected by the thick line of trees shading the creek.

"I'm finding out this is actually pretty typical of isolated Western towns," he replied. "There's no sprawl. The edge of town is just that." He made a chopping motion. "The edge of town."

"Yet there must be some development further away,"

she said. "Like the bid you made earlier for your new clients—didn't you say they were on the other side of town on a parcel of land?"

"*Ja*, there is some private ownership. But a lot of what surrounds Pierce is either farmland or ranchland, without many buildings."

"I wonder..." She hesitated, then plunged on. "If there is as little development as you say, how can your business succeed? It seems you're limiting yourself in how far you can travel to take a job if you can only use a horse and buggy."

He frowned. She had unwittingly pinpointed one of his greatest areas of concern. "I don't know. It may be. One of the men working for me is *Englisch* and has his own pickup truck and logging truck, so I pay him extra when he drives his vehicles to a jobsite. It's just too hard to transport logs for a log home without a big truck, of course, but one of the homes we're building is several miles outside of town, and it's more efficient to get there in Peter's pickup truck."

"Does the bishop have an issue with that?"

He was surprised she would know to ask such a question. "I've talked with him about it. He understands the need in a business context, as long as it doesn't interfere with the cohesion of the community. I've worked hard to make sure that's the case."

"Then why are you beating yourself up over using trucks?"

He gave a grim chuckle. "You're right, that's exactly what I've been doing. And I should stop, I know. It's just that—that I've never been in business for myself before. There are so many different factors to consider." He paused and added, "Sometimes I think I did the wrong thing, starting my own business."

She looked surprised. "It's not going well?"

He shrugged, not wanting to admit his financial status. "It's doing okay."

"Adam, let me ask you a personal question. Is it a financial hardship to employ me as Lucas's nanny?"

"Any start-up business has its growing pains," he hedged. "But the fact that I can now concentrate without worrying about my son is a huge benefit."

She looked unconvinced, and he suspected she could guess the state of his financial affairs.

"And as you say, one of the weaknesses is I'm limited to just local work, unless I want to be away from Lucas overnight," he continued. "And I'll admit, I have a hard time managing some of the business aspects. Bids and quotes and estimates, that kind of thing. I'm more comfortable working with my hands and I can see in my mind's eye how a project should unfold, but customers want hard numbers and accurate estimates."

"I see." She looked thoughtful, her eyes on Lucas as the child examined something along the edge of the path ahead of them. "You once mentioned you regret moving to Montana. Sounds like those regrets are still with you."

"Sometimes, *ja*." He rubbed his chin. "Many of those regrets have to do with Lucas. I simply didn't factor in how much I depended on having help with his care by a lot of the older women in the community who stepped in when my wife passed away. It's mostly a younger group who emigrated here to Montana to found this new church, and it's been a rather intense few years as everyone scrambles to build homes and farms and businesses. I haven't been able to find anyone dependable to watch my son."

"I can see why that's a problem." She kept her eyes on the child. "Then you're right, maybe my car breaking down here *was* God's plan." She turned and smiled at him.

His breath caught. There was no doubt that Ruth was a lovely young woman.

But he didn't dare let the moment turn into something inappropriate. Ruth was not of his faith. He strove to keep his response businesslike. "That's my opinion, too," he began, and was relieved when Lucas dashed over to show them the large bird feather he'd found.

"It's big!" the child exclaimed.

"Wow, it certainly is!" Ruth took the feather, which was at least twelve inches in length. "What kind of bird is this from, do you suppose?"

"Wild turkey," he answered. "They're everywhere. We see flocks of them pass by the house all the time."

"Can you fly with this one feather?" she asked Lucas, handing him back the item.

The child giggled and dashed about, flapping and jumping. "I'm a bird! I'm a bird!"

"Your *Deutsch* is improving," he remarked. "And ironically, Lucas's English is improving, too."

"I'm remembering a lot more than I thought I could," she agreed, continuing the stroll. "I confess, I've been practicing it on Lucas while I'm caring for him."

"It's *gut* for him to learn *Englisch*, too," Adam remarked.

A silence fell between them for a few moments. Then, out of the blue, Ruth said, "You know, I'm pretty good with numbers. If you need help putting together bids or estimates, I can lend a hand. If you want."

He was so startled by this offer that he stopped in his tracks. "You can?"

"Sure." She paused and looked at him. "I worked with a lot of numbers in my last job. I'm fairly good with them. I don't know anything about construction, but you can show me how best to put a bid together and I can crunch the numbers for you."

He felt a surge of relief at the thought of handing over a hated task to someone who seemed more competent. He scrubbed a hand over his face and resumed walking. "I might just take you up on that," he confessed. "It's the one part of running a business I hate doing. My foreman suggested I might have to hire someone, and I agree. If you can help me with this, I'll compensate you."

"You don't have to…" she began.

He waved her to silence. "*Ja*, of course I would pay you. Otherwise I'd have to pay someone else, ain't so?" Curiosity got the better of him, and he asked, "What did you do in your last job that you're so *gut* with numbers?"

"Finance." Her face went blank and she kept her eyes on Lucas as he dashed around. "I—I wasn't very good at my job, but I have no problem working with numbers."

He wanted to find out why she thought she wasn't good at her job. Instinct told him the air of mystery about her had something to do with her job, and he wondered what could possibly have sent her careening across the country with no goal and no destination.

But he couldn't argue, because she had so far been a blessing. First Lucas, and now her skills with numbers. He wasn't inclined to look a gift horse in the mouth.

He glanced at the sun. "I guess we should start back. Lucas hasn't had his nap yet, so if I'm smart I'll make sure he gets some downtime."

"Good idea." He noted both her remark and her expression were neutral.

He called Lucas back and started on the return path toward town. He had a nagging feeling he was avoiding delving into whatever secrets Ruth had in her past because he didn't want to disturb the present.

He hoped that decision wouldn't come back to haunt him later.

Chapter Eight

"And that's all there is to it. Easy peasy." With a grin, Ruth slid a notebook across the table toward Adam.

"Says you," he retorted with a grin of his own. "I'm just glad it's done."

The slim folder held a completed estimate for building the log cabin for the Johnsons, the family Adam had spoken to shortly after Ruth started working for him.

It was the culmination of a rather intense week of collaboration. Adam had given Ruth a crash course on the components of estimates, bids and proposals. In return, she had coached him on accounting and bookkeeping. Working mostly during Lucas's naptimes, Ruth included all the attributes Adam said were necessary for a proper document. She made sure she triple-checked all the numbers and had the estimate completed by Friday.

"Do you think the Johnsons will quibble on the cost?" she asked.

"I don't think so. They seem fairly certain this is what they want, and they didn't strike me as overly frugal.

Not affluent, mind you, but not doing badly. Also…"
He gave a rueful chuckle. "…I think they like the idea
of an Amish team doing the construction. I suppose
it's novel."

"It is, out here." She caught his humor. "Now that I
have an idea of how to do these, I don't mind working
on more as they come up. Who knows, it might become
a side line of work I can consider."

"There's always a need for people to do this kind
of stuff. And I, for one, thank you. I'm more comfortable working with my hands. I've never been a numbers man, so this saves me a tremendous amount of
stress. And this little man…" Adam reached down to
pull Lucas into his lap. "…has been a *gut* boy, letting
us get all this silly paperwork done. What do you say,
Lucas? Want to come to the log yard with me tomorrow?"

"Ja!" The child bounced up and down. "Can I hammer something?"

"Ja, sure. You can help me put up some siding, too."

Watching them together, Ruth smiled. It was clear
Lucas was a miniature version of his father—obsessed
with tools and their uses, always wanting to build and
construct and create.

Ruth also knew why Adam chose tomorrow to take
Lucas to the log yard: it was Saturday, and the place
would be quiet. There was far less of a chance for an
active boy to get in trouble.

"What will you do tomorrow?" Adam asked, turning his attention to her.

"Well, actually, Nell Peachey offered to show me

how to make cheese," she admitted. "I've been curious about the process for quite some time, so she volunteered to show me. And Eva Hostetler, she said she would teach me how to can. Not tomorrow, of course, but maybe the Saturday after. I can use some of the vegetables from your garden, if that's all right."

"Use all you want." Adam waved a hand. "Sometimes it's hard to keep up with the garden as it is. But why the interest in canning and cheese making?"

Ruth was aware of the unspoken question that hovered in the air: What good would these domestic skills serve her in a New York City apartment?

She spoke slowly. "I don't know. It's almost as if— as if watching Nell and Eva has awakened something long dormant inside me. I know my mother used to preserve food and make cheese, though she stopped after we left the community."

She felt like blinking back tears when he asked, "Do you remember your parents clearly?"

"Bits and pieces." She picked at the edge of the notebook. "Being back here with an Amish group has stirred up a lot more memories than I thought. I find myself remembering many little things—the way my father's voice sounded, the tune of one of the hymns we used to sing…and more and more of the language."

"You remember some of the hymns?" His eyebrows rose. "That's impressive, considering how young you were."

"I remember some of the *tunes*. I don't remember the words."

"You should come to a church service and see if the words come back to you."

She stilled. It was an idea she had been kicking around anyway—attending a service. Seeing how much she remembered. Hearing the old familiar hymns. Enjoying the camaraderie of the meal afterward…

"Do—do you think I'd be welcome?" she quavered.

"Why wouldn't you be? We've had visitors before, and besides, you were raised Amish. Seems to me it would be a natural step."

"Step toward what?" she blurted.

He shrugged, she thought, a bit evasively. "Forgive me for getting personal, but I get the impression you're kind of groping, spiritually. Am I wrong?"

"No," she said slowly, "you're not wrong. It's just strange. I haven't given much thought to faith for a long, long time. Not since my parents died. Losing them didn't exactly make me question the existence of God, but in the aftermath I didn't receive any spiritual comfort, either. But I have to admit, I've been reading parts of the Bible the Millers left in my room."

He bounced Lucas gently on his lap. "I can pick you up and take you to church this Sunday, if you like. Or you might be able to hitch a ride with the Millers."

"Since I'm right there, I'm sure they wouldn't mind." For the first time in a long time, though, she considered her clothes. Her wardrobe was decidedly un-Amish. "Should I dress the part, do you suppose?"

"I wouldn't worry about it. Everyone knows you're watching Lucas for me, and I suspect word has gotten round that you were raised Amish as a kid. I think you'd be very welcome."

She felt a blooming warmth inside, a longing to connect with a unified community. "I'll talk to Anna this evening," she decided.

It wasn't until she was biking back toward town that she considered Adam's suggestion to attend a church service in a different light. While he seemed unusually attuned toward her spiritual need, she wondered if he had an ulterior motive.

She thought about him—the way his blue eyes crinkled when he laughed, the way his curly hair tended to get flattened under his hat. She enjoyed his company. In many respects, they were very compatible. He was a good father, a good provider for his son. Plus, he was a widower and doubtless felt some interest in her as a single woman caring for his child. But as a baptized member of the church, he could not pursue that path because she didn't share his faith.

Was that why he'd invited her to a worship service?

Yet, aside from any potential clandestine cause on Adam's part, his offer was welcome. She wanted to go.

"To a church service?" clarified Anna Miller that evening, when Ruth proposed the possibility. "*Ja*, sure. I see no problem with that. We have room in our buggy, so you can ride with us."

"Yes, that's what Adam suggested."

Anna's eyebrows elevated. "This was Adam's suggestion?"

"Um, yeah." To her annoyance, Ruth felt herself blush. Anna's unspoken conclusion was obvious. "It's not what you think," she added hastily. "I just happened to mention how some of my childhood memories are starting to come back, including hymns. But I don't remember the words, just some of the tunes. He thought I might like to refresh my memory, so to speak, by attending a service."

"I see." A tiny smile quirked the side of the older woman's mouth. "I've heard you playing one of our regular hymns on your guitar. I'm sure you'll remember it the moment you hear it."

"It's kind of funny, what snippets are coming back to me. But yes, if you have room in your buggy on Sunday, I would very much like a ride."

"*Ja,* sure." Anna smiled. "We'll leave around eight thirty."

The next day, while visiting Nell Peachey and learning the intricacies of cheese making, Ruth mentioned she would be attending church. Unlike Anna, however, Nell didn't seem to pick up on any potential matchmaking overtones with Adam.

"*Ach*, how lovely!" she exclaimed in genuine delight. "If you'd like to sit with me as my guest, you'd be *welkom*."

"I will, thank you!" Ruth felt warmed by the woman's enthusiasm. "That way I won't feel like a fish out of water. Especially since I won't be dressed properly."

"There are no fish out of water in *Gott*'s house," said Nell, handing Ruth a slotted spoon and indicating she should stir rennet into the milk. "And you'll be dressed just fine. Your *Deutsch* is improving, so you'll be able to follow the service."

When Ruth returned to the boardinghouse later that

afternoon, she brought with her a two-pound chunk of freshly made mozzarella cheese for the Millers. She had learned a lot that week—how to create a construction estimate, how to make cheese—and, perhaps, how to remember a little more of her lost childhood.

"Stay close by me," Adam instructed his son as he unhitched the horse. Holding the animal's bridle in one hand, he took Lucas's hand in the other and led the animal toward the shady corral where the other horses were kept during the church service.

The Amish community was sedate and solemn as they walked or rode in buggies toward the Stoltzfuses' farm, which had a large new barn often used for services. Back in Indiana, Church Sundays rotated among different farms so no one got too overwhelmed by continuous hosting, but here in Montana, most people were still building up their infrastructure, and somehow the Stoltzfus family had, by default, become the favored hosts. They were good-natured about it, and everyone pitched in extra hard to make sure they were not swamped with work.

He tried not to look around for Ruth, but he hoped she would come. He hadn't said anything to Lucas, since he suspected most of the conversation that happened two days before had gone over the little boy's head. He didn't want to get the child's hopes up.

But there she was, riding in the back of the buggy with the Millers, looking around her with avid interest. He had to admit, his heart sped up when he saw her. If he wasn't careful, he could easily become just as enamored of Ruth as Lucas was.

Lucas, busy waving to friends, hadn't noticed his nanny's arrival. Adam tried not to track Ruth's progress, but through the corner of his eyes, he watched as she climbed down from the buggy and walked with Anna toward the spacious barn where the service was being held.

She stuck out like a sore thumb among the crowd, though her clothing was as subdued as he'd ever seen it—a midcalf-length black skirt, a dark green blouse and a black kerchief over her hair. She chatted animatedly with Anna.

He saw Eva Hostetler break away from her family and go greet Ruth. He smiled to himself. With two such pillars of the community—Anna and her daughter Eva—Ruth would receive as warm a welcome as he could hope.

"*Komm*, Lucas, the men are gathering," he told his son. He took a firmer grip on the boy's hand and began walking toward the barn.

"Miss Ruth!" With surprising strength, Lucas wrenched his hand free and darted toward his nanny.

"Lucas!" called Adam, annoyed. It embarrassed him to see his impulsive son misbehave, especially on a Church Sunday.

The boy catapulted himself at Ruth, knocking her back a step or two as he barreled into her legs. He heard her laugh as she bent down to pick him up and give him a hug.

As Adam made his way over to retrieve his son, he had to admit it was a nice excuse to talk with her.

"I'm sorry," he apologized. "He just yanked his hand out of mine when he saw you."

"Were you being naughty?" she asked Lucas with a twinkle in her eye. "You shouldn't have run away from your *dat*."

"*Ja*, I know." The child had an extraordinary blend of regret and mirth on his face. He looked over at Adam. "I'm sorry, *Dat*."

Adam stretched out his arms to take the child back. "Let Miss Ruth alone now, *sohn*. She's here to worship, just like we are."

"Lucas, would you like to eat lunch with me after the service?" Ruth asked, and the boy immediately brightened.

Adam recaptured his son's hand as he headed for the barn. He tried to keep calm, but he was just as delighted as Lucas was to eat the midday meal with Ruth. Yes, he was becoming besotted with the woman. He admitted it to himself, if no one else.

While singing a hymn, he snuck a peek at Ruth. Her eyes were closed, a look of delight on her face, and she was singing. He smiled to himself. So she remembered the words.

This newly discovered infatuation made it difficult for him to focus on the sermon, during which—ironically—the bishop spoke of self-control. Adam tried to clamp down on his emotions. He knew Ruth was out of his league. She was not Amish and she had not spoken of any plans to stay once her commitment with Lucas was over. It was foolish to become interested in her.

After the service concluded, he filed out of the men's

side of the barn and kept his hand firmly around his son's. "Don't go running off," he warned.

"But Miss Ruth—she's right there!" argued Lucas, tugging.

"Let Miss Ruth have a moment to herself, *sohn*." He smiled behind his firm words. "At least wait until she has a plate of food, *ja*?"

"Ja," Lucas agreed in a sulky voice.

Back in Indiana, there were so many people attending church that the meals were served in shifts. Here, there were far fewer people and the potluck was more informal. Family groups or friends sat with each other. He kept Lucas by his side, letting Ruth fill her plate, before allowing his son to choose his own meal. He knew the boy was hungry and less likely to bother Ruth if he could focus on food.

But then, balancing a plate in each hand, he watched as Lucas inevitably made a beeline for Ruth, who was sitting at a picnic table nearby with the Millers and the Hostetlers. Ruth smiled at the child and made room on the bench for him to sit.

He walked up. *"Guder nammidaag.* May I join you?"

"Of course," said Anna, scooting over on the bench to make room. "Although Lucas beat you here."

"Hungry!" announced the boy.

"I know. Don't forget to say a blessing," reminded Adam as he put one plate on the table before the boy.

Lucas bowed his head and closed his eyes, and concluded his prayer with remarkable speed before cramming a biscuit in his mouth.

Ruth chuckled. "Good appetite," she remarked.

"How goes the log home business?" asked Eli Miller from across the table.

Adam knew he was unlikely to get a private word in with Ruth anyway, so he resigned himself to discussing business with Eli while Anna and Eva chattered with Ruth, and Lucas stuffed himself with a speed Adam hoped would not become cause for regret later that evening.

Ruth glanced at Lucas. "Slow down!" she admonished with a smile on her face. "The food isn't going anywhere."

"I want to go play with Jacob," replied Lucas indistinctly, his mouth full.

"Jacob is still eating, too, see?" She pointed.

But her rebuke made little difference. Lucas cleaned his plate with notable speed. "Can I go now?" he asked.

Adam chuckled. "*Ja*, you can go. I see Jacob is finished, too. Don't go near the horses, though."

Lucas climbed off the picnic bench with alacrity, and Adam watched as he dashed over to join his friend. "Go go go," he remarked. "I wish I had that much energy."

"I suspect he'll crash this afternoon for his nap," Ruth said.

Eli once again engaged him in business conversation, and half an hour passed in leisurely talk before Adam thought to keep track of the child.

He looked around. "Where did Lucas go?"

A sudden shout of voices made him snap his head around. People didn't shout on the Sabbath, unless...

A shrill scream from several women, shouts from some men, a sickening thud, and he felt the blood drain from his face. Instinct told him the commotion involved his son.

He shoved back from the picnic table so fast he almost knocked Anna over. Dashing to where the crowd had gathered under a tree, he pushed random people aside until he saw little Lucas, his straw hat knocked off, crumpled on the ground. Fear clutched his midsection. "Lucas!"

The dissonant voices around him buzzed in his ear as he knelt beside the boy. "Fell from a tree…"

"Fell off that branch…"

"Climbed too high…"

The child's eyes fluttered open, their dark depths full of pain. But it wasn't until Adam tried to lift Lucas up that the child screamed, and Adam saw Lucas's left arm was twisted in an unnatural position. He swallowed down some bile at the horrible sight.

"We're going to the hospital," said a firm voice in his ear. He realized Ruth was at his side. "I'll hold him. Go hitch up the buggy."

He nodded and gently lifted Lucas to transfer him into her arms. The child leaned into her chest, perhaps too shocked to cry anymore, and seemed to take some comfort.

Eli Miller had clearly anticipated the situation and was already hitching the right horse to the right buggy. Within moments, Adam was able to swing into the seat, nodding his thanks to the older man. He turned the horse and bumped the buggy over the grass toward where everyone clustered around Ruth holding Lucas.

"Don't speed too fast," advised one of the gray-beards. "Jostling will hurt him worse."

"*Ja*, you're right." Adam paused a moment with a hand to his chest, then straightened again. "Can you come?" he asked Ruth. "He trusts you."

"Of course. Lucas, darling, I'm going to let this nice man hold you while I get into the buggy, okay? Then I'll hold you while we take you to the hospital."

He nodded weakly. Adam swallowed hard as his son started crying when Ruth transferred him to the *gross-daddi*. She jumped into the buggy, and the old man laid the child in her arms. "*Gott* be with you," he intoned.

Adam nodded his thanks, turned the buggy, and made his way toward town.

Chapter Nine

Ruth had not considered herself religious for so long that she felt as if she'd forgotten how to pray. But seeing Lucas crumpled on the ground, screaming in pain, caused her to pray as she had never prayed before.

Adam was grimly silent, directing the horse at a fast trot on the road toward town. Ruth clasped Lucas's little body against her, trying not to touch his broken arm. She heard him catching his breath in little kitten-like mews of pain, but otherwise he was silent. Eerily silent.

"Please God…" she begged noiselessly, her thoughts chaotic and incoherent.

She started humming to him, the tune of one of the hymns they had just sung. She came to the end and looped around to the beginning, over and over, desperate to soothe the child any way she could.

The grassy fields quickly transitioned into the town. Traffic was light since it was a Sunday. Adam kept the horse at a brisk clip, and Ruth was grateful the town's only traffic light was green for them. Adam turned right, down a side street, when the tiny hospital came into view. Ruth didn't think she was ever as glad to see a sign as she was to see the one that read Emergency Entrance, in red letters.

"Stay here, I'll go get someone," he told her, yanking the panting horse to a halt.

He had barely jumped down from the buggy when two orderlies came out, looking questioningly at the horse and buggy.

"My son fell out of a tree and broke his arm," Adam croaked. "Please, we need help."

The two men nodded without a word and disappeared inside, only to reappear within moments with a gurney. They wheeled it beside the buggy and reached up to take Lucas from her arms.

The boy started to cry as the taller of the orderlies gently transferred him to the gurney and the shorter man strapped him in. *"Dat,"* he cried. *"Dat..."*

"I'm here, Lucas." Adam bent over the gurney. Without a word or a backward look, he ran alongside his son and disappeared indoors.

Left alone, Ruth climbed out of the buggy and walked up to the horse. "You did good," she whispered to the animal, petting her and stroking her nose. She had no idea how to unhitch the horse or even where the buggy should be parked, so she stayed by the horse's head at the entrance. And she prayed.

Half an hour elapsed. Rummaging in the buggy, Ruth found a livestock brush and started to brush the horse, working around the animal's collar and straps, down her legs, across her flanks. The horse's head drooped and she half closed her eyes at the pleasurable sensation. Meanwhile, Ruth continued to pray.

"I forgot all about the horse."

Startled, she looked around. Adam had walked out of the building's double doors. His face looked drawn and haggard.

"How's Lucas?"

"Getting his arm cast. I was able to be with him while they took X-rays—they had to make sure he didn't have a concussion or some other injury—but it was just his arm. They asked me to stay in the waiting room while they put his arm in a cast. According to them it was a clean break and will heal well." He scrubbed a hand over his face. "I think he scared ten years off my life today," he added.

"I know the feeling," she muttered. She gave the horse a final pat and put the brush back in the buggy.

"Ruth…"

Surprised at his tone of voice—almost intimate— she jerked her head around.

"*Vielen Dank* for coming with me. I couldn't have done this alone." His eyes held an unfathomable expression.

"There are lots of people who could have come along," she reminded him, trying not to read too much into his gratitude.

"But none whom Lucas trusted as much. Thanks to you, he stayed quiet all the way to town. Parenting is very much a two-person job," he added under his breath.

Not quite certain how to reply, she simply patted the

horse. "How much longer will Lucas be inside? And what should we do with the horse until he's finished?"

Her questions seemed to stir Adam from his dazed worry. He shook his head, as if snapping himself awake, and looked around. "Not much by way of hitching posts," he noted. "But there's an empty parking lot across the street—" He pointed. "I can direct Maggie there and tie her up to the tree. That way we're not taking up this parking area and she'll have shade while we wait."

She stood back while he climbed into the buggy and guided the horse across the street. It took him just a few moments to secure the animal to the tree. She saw him pat the animal's neck before crossing back to the hospital building.

Inside, they were the only ones in the waiting room. A television silently broadcast a news show, but Ruth paid no attention. She leafed through magazines that didn't interest her in the slightest. Her entire focus was on what might be happening to Lucas, somewhere in the hospital. Was he crying? Terrified? In pain?

Beside her, Adam didn't even pretend to interest himself in the reading material. He sat, hands clenched, staring at the closed doors. Ruth was under the impression he was praying, but he said nothing.

An hour ticked away, until finally a doctor pushed through the double doors. "Mr. Chupp?"

"Ja." Adam bounced to his feet.

"I'm Dr. Rodriguez," he replied, shaking Adam's hand. "Are you Mrs. Chupp?" he inquired, turning toward Ruth.

"No, I'm just the nanny," she replied.

"Is your name Ruth, then?"

"Yes." She lifted her eyebrows in inquiry.

The doctor gave a dry chuckle. "Lucas has been talking about his *'dat'* and a 'Miss Ruth.' I guess that's you."

"My wife passed away when Lucas was a baby," Adam explained in a hurry. "But Lucas—how is he?"

"Fine. As breaks go, this wasn't bad. We only had to cast his arm below the elbow, so he'll be able to stay fairly active. My own son broke his arm at about the same age, and since he broke the humerus—" the doctor made a chopping motion toward his upper arm "—he had a much larger cast that limited his mobility. It was quite an ordeal."

"And Lucas has no concussion?"

"No. He has some bruising, of course, and he'll be in pain for several days. We'll send him home with pain medication. And please try to keep him as quiet as possible."

For the first time since the accident, Adam cracked a smile. "That's how he broke his arm in the first place. I can't keep him quiet. My son is a firecracker—always moving."

The doctor smiled back, his dark eyes sympathetic. "I have three sons—all grown now—so I fully understand. Still, do your best. He's likely to sleep a fair bit over the next couple of days, at least. Breaking a bone can really be exhausting, especially for someone as young as Lucas."

"When can I take him home?"

"In a few minutes." With a smile, the doctor disappeared down the hallway again.

Adam collapsed in one of the chairs. "Keep him quiet," he muttered. "An impossible task."

Ruth felt like giving him a hug, he was so distraught, but it would not have been appropriate. Instead she, too, perched on a chair. The clock ticked by.

Finally, after what seemed like forever, the double doors opened and a nurse appeared, pushing Lucas in a wheelchair. The child looked pale, but he was smiling bravely, cradling his cast arm on his lap. "*Dat!* Miss Ruth!"

Adam catapulted toward the boy and dropped to one knee in front of him. "Am I glad to see you!"

"*Ja.* I want to go home." The boy's bottom lip trembled.

"We'll go straight home, don't worry."

"The doctor gave me this to give to you." The nurse held out a vial of pills. "Twice a day. If he's in extra pain, you might give him a third, but no more than four over twenty-four hours."

"*Ja*, thank you. And thank you for taking care of my son."

"Why don't you go get the horse and buggy?" suggested Ruth. "I'll stay with Lucas."

Adam nodded, touched his son's cheek, then turned and walked out of the hospital.

Ruth squatted down next to the boy. "I won't pretend we weren't scared," she told him. "I think you're off tree-climbing duty for an hour or two, okay?"

"*Ja*, okay," the child agreed. He tossed his head. "But the nurse said I'm brave."

Ruth glanced up at the nurse, who shrugged and

smiled. "But not so brave that you should tackle another tree right away," the nurse suggested.

"Here comes your *dat*," said Ruth, standing up. She looked at the nurse. "Can he walk?"

"We'll wheel him straight out to the car, er, the buggy," the nurse said. "But yes, he'll be able to walk."

As Adam pulled the horse and buggy under the portico of the Emergency Room entrance, Ruth walked next to Lucas's wheelchair while the nurse pushed it out the doors.

"Let me climb in, then he can sit on my lap," she told the nurse.

Within a few moments, Lucas was on her lap. "What do you say to the nice lady?" she whispered to the boy.

Lucas peered around at the nurse. *"Danke,"* he said with a smile.

The nurse smiled and waved. "We'll see you in a few weeks to get your cast off."

After a flurry of thank-yous and goodbyes, Adam clucked to the horse and the animal clopped at a leisurely pace through the quiet streets of the town.

Adam heaved an enormous sigh. He could almost feel new gray hairs sprouting on his head as they headed away from the hospital. It wasn't the first time Lucas had gotten into a serious scrape, and he knew it wouldn't be the last. The thought that had rocketed through his mind when he saw Lucas on the ground at church was that he had failed his wife. Lucas was running wild. But short of harsh restrictions, Adam wasn't sure what to do about it.

Directing the horse through town, he prayed for peace. There were times—dark and desperate times—when he honestly wondered whether he shouldn't give Lucas away to another family, rather than trying to raise the child as a single dad. This was one of those moments.

"Do you want to just drop me off at the boarding-house?" suggested Ruth.

"*Ja*, sure." He glanced at her, sitting so sedately next to him with his injured son on her lap. The black kerchief over her hair almost resembled a *kapp*. Lucas had his head pressed against her chest with his eyes closed. At that moment, Adam wondered if *Gott* was talking to him directly—something he would have to analyze later.

Within a few minutes, he pulled up to the boarding-house. Ruth kissed Lucas, who clung to her for a moment, then carefully handed the boy to Adam while she climbed out. As Adam settled Lucas into the vacant seat, Ruth turned and brushed a lock of hair off Lucas's forehead. "I'll see you tomorrow, okay?"

"*Ja*," replied the boy.

"Ruth…" Adam swallowed, suddenly tongue-tied. "I have much to thank you for." The words seemed inadequate, but they were all he could come up with.

She nodded. "Tomorrow," she confirmed, then turned and went inside.

Adam directed the horse out of town and toward the farm. He glanced at Lucas. "Are you in much pain right now?"

"A little," the boy replied. He touched his cast. "This feels funny."

"The good news is you can draw on your cast," he told his son. "Your friends can draw funny pictures on it too."

"Really?" The boy brightened. "Jacob's *mamm*—she draws nice pictures. Maybe she can draw me a dog."

"I'm sure she'd love to." He tousled his son's hair. "You gave me quite a scare, *sohn*. Miss Ruth is right. No more climbing trees for a while, *ja*?"

"Ja, Dat."

By the time they got home and Adam had unhitched and stabled the horse, he could tell the child was in pain as well as exhausted. He gave Lucas some of the pain medicine the doctor had given him, then tucked the boy into bed and dropped a kiss on his forehead. Lucas was asleep in moments.

Adam took advantage of that to get some barn chores done. He fed and watered the cows, the horse and the chickens. He had just finished gathering eggs when he heard a buggy approach. Peering around the edge of the building, he saw the bishop, Samuel Beiler, pulling his horse to a stop before the front gate as Buster bounced around, wagging his tail. The man's iron-gray hair was visible under his straw hat.

Adam called the dog to his side and went to greet the church leader. "*Guder nammidaag*, Bishop."

"Whoa," the older man told his horse. "*Guder nammidaag*, Adam. I came to see how Lucas is doing."

"It turns out he broke his forearm, though fortunately he didn't have a concussion. He's asleep at the moment with a cast on his arm. Won't you come in for a bit? I wouldn't mind sitting down. It's been a stressful afternoon."

"Ja, danke." The older man climbed out of his buggy and tied his horse to a tree.

Adam was able to produce two glasses of cool lemonade, and invited the bishop to sit on the porch while he told him about Lucas's hospital visit.

"Sometimes I wonder if I'm doing right by my boy," concluded Adam with a sigh. "I often wonder how different things would be if Bethany had lived."

"Young children need a mother's touch," affirmed the bishop. "Adam, have you given any thought to remarrying?"

"Whom could I marry?" he replied with unexpected bitterness. "It was something I didn't anticipate when I moved out here—the lack of women my age. There is no widow around, no woman who would be interested in a built-in family with an older man. Anyone who is unmarried here is still a *youngie.*"

"Is there no one back in Indiana…?" prompted the bishop.

"Nein. No one. Bethany was the only one for me."

The bishop sighed. "Sometimes I worry about you, Adam. You're lonely."

"Of course I'm lonely," snapped Adam. "That's what being widowed is all about."

"Your new nanny seems to have a soft spot for Lucas," Bishop Beiler said, changing the subject.

Startled, Adam stared at the man. "Ruth? But she isn't Amish."

"Yet." The older man smiled.

Adam was floored. The bishop was acting as matchmaker? For a woman who wasn't Amish? "Samuel, what are you suggesting, exactly? That I try and convince Ruth to convert and become baptized? That's not our way. We don't evangelize."

"Sometimes, Adam, I think there are special cases. This may be one of them. You seem very fond of her."

"Maybe I am, but it hardly matters. She's not of our faith, and I won't push her to join. We believe in letting our light shine, but we don't spotlight it in the eyes of other people."

"Perhaps not, but Ruth strikes me as something of an exception. She was raised Amish, ain't so? And she fit in very well at the church service today. I've heard both Nell Peachey and Eva Hostetler mention how easily she seems to slip into our ways. It seems to me she might be a soul who is searching for a home, both literal and spiritual."

Adam rubbed his forehead. "This is quite an unexpected turn..."

"Are you telling me you've never entertained the idea that Ruth might have a place in your future?"

"I won't go that far," Adam admitted with a small smile. "All I have to do is watch how much Lucas adores her, and the thought flickers through my mind. We seem to get along easily. But there's some sort of mystery about her. She had something of a traumatic childhood—her parents left the church, then they were killed in a car accident not long after. She had a difficult time as a young teen, especially after her parents died. She was raised in a foster family."

The bishop waved a hand. "None of those things are her fault."

"Of course not. But there's something more recent, something strange she refuses to talk about that sent her on a cross-country trip. I don't know, Bishop…she seems very impulsive to me."

"And yet, you like her." It was a statement, not a question.

"Of course I like her," returned Adam. "How could I not? But it's a far stretch between liking my son's nanny and wanting to marry her."

Samuel chuckled, and Adam was uneasily aware that he was protesting too much at the thought of a future with Ruth—because, of course, that very idea *had* been on his mind a lot.

"Well, as you say, she isn't Amish." Samuel took a sip of his lemonade, then added, "Both Eva Hostetler and her mother, Anna, seem to like Ruth very much."

"And Nell Peachy," added Adam. "Nell is teaching her how to make cheese, and Eva offered to show her how to can vegetables. Ruth does seem interested in recapturing some of the Amish skills she remembers her own mother possessing."

"Interesting," said the bishop. "So, if Ruth were Amish, is she someone you would consider courting?"

Adam paused for a moment. *"Ja,"* he admitted. "But I would not want to leave the church to marry her," he added hastily. "I don't want to do anything in violation of my baptismal vows."

The church leader nodded. "I understand the barriers between you and Ruth all too well. But some gentle persuasion to lead her into our church might be in order."

Adam heaved a great sigh. "To be honest, Samuel, nothing you've said is anything I haven't already thought about," he acknowledged. "When Lucas can't stop talking about her, when he turns to her for comfort when he's hurt, when he pesters mc to go see her on weekends—well, it's hard not to take that extra leap of logic and wonder if she would make a *gut* mother. Or a *gut* wife."

"It's almost as if Lucas has chosen her already," observed the bishop.

Again, Adam was surprised by the older man's discernment. *"Ja,"* he agreed. "I've considered that, too. I've never seen him warm up like this to any other caregiver. He's obsessed with her."

"And are you?" pursued the bishop.

Adam grimaced. "I try not to be."

"That's what I thought." Samuel chuckled. "Well, it's as *Gott* wills. For my part, if Ruth shows an interest in joining the church, I'd be more than happy to guide her."

"Danke," replied Adam with a ghost of a smile. "As you say, whatever happens will be *Gott*'s will."

Samuel drained the last of his lemonade and rose to his feet. "Well, I'd best get home. Lois was anxious to know how your boy was doing, so I'll let her know he'll recover."

Adam walked Samuel back to his buggy and watched as the older man drove away. So the bishop wanted him to marry Ruth, did he?

While he had told Samuel the truth—that he would welcome the opportunity to court her if she was of the same faith—he knew the chances of that happening were slim. She had too much *Englisch* in her. He knew it was dramatically difficult for someone not raised Amish—at least not during their formative years—to give up the temptations and modern conveniences of the wider world.

While Ruth seemed unfazed to be caring for Lucas in a home without electricity, he knew it was a big leap to go from a job to a lifestyle.

He wandered back inside the house and peeked in at Lucas, who still slept. Adam had a feeling he would be up quite a bit tonight as the child wrestled with pain. In a way, he welcomed the vigil.

It would keep Lucas's nanny out of his thoughts.

Chapter Ten

When Ruth arrived at the Chupp farm on her bicycle the next morning, Buster bounced around at the gate, but all else was quiet. Normally Adam was there to greet her, or Lucas watched for her on the porch. Even the usual barnyard sounds seemed subdued. Puzzled at the silence, Ruth let herself into the house.

Adam was sprawled in a recliner chair, with Lucas lying across his lap. Father and son were fast asleep and didn't so much as stir an eyelash at her entry.

Lucas's cheek rested on Adam's shirt in an attitude of utter trust. It was clear Adam had been up with Lucas most of the night, and only recently had managed sleep for either of them. The tender way Adam had Lucas in his arms spoke of his effort to comfort a child in pain.

She tiptoed into the kitchen and started to put together biscuits and gravy for a hot breakfast, trying to be as quiet as possible. It took twenty minutes alone to bake the biscuits, and neither father nor son stirred that whole time. When the meal was ready, Adam and Lucas were still sound asleep.

She wondered briefly if she should just go home, but some instinct told her Lucas would need her today. Instead she went outdoors, where the bright fall day smelled sweet and crisp.

A subdued clucking and crowing from the chicken coop caught her attention. Evidently the poultry were still inside their coop from the evening before, since she knew Adam locked them in at night. Had Adam not yet done his barn chores?

Ruth entered the pen and unlatched the coop door, and the restless birds spilled out into their yard. She filled their feeder, gave them fresh water, then gathered the eggs in a basket Adam kept on a hook near the coop door and brought them back to the kitchen.

Still Adam and Lucas slept.

She put the eggs in a bowl and wondered if Adam had yet milked the cow. The clean steel bucket and lid he normally used was still upended in the drain rack, so she suspected the answer was no. She wondered if she could tackle that chore herself. She hadn't milked a cow since she was eleven years old, but had enjoyed it when she was a child. Could she milk a cow again?

Bucket in one hand and a bowl of water with a clean cloth in the other, she made her way to the barn. The two cows swished their tails irritably in their stalls, anxious to get to their calves who were separated by a stout rail fence. The calves bleated, hungry. Ruth knew Adam milked just once a day. He separated the babies at night, milked in the morning, then let mothers and calves stay together the rest of the day.

The milking setup was clean and obvious. Ruth snapped a lead rope to the halter of one of the cows and led her into the milking stall. A plastic crate was hooked on a nail on the wall, so Ruth used it as a milking stool. She sat down, washed off the udder and began zinging warm milk into the steel pail.

Her old skill came right back to her. Ruth smiled as she pressed her forehead against the cow's warm flank. It was like riding a bicycle—she didn't forget. She remembered the pride she'd felt when she was old enough to tackle that chore as a child. She grinned wider at the thought of surprising Adam and getting his barn chores done.

Fifteen minutes later, the pail was full of foamy milk and the cow's udder was empty. Ruth snapped the lid on the pail, backed the cow out of the milking stall and led her to the corral. Then she released the calf, who darted to her mother's side and began vigorously nursing. Ruth smiled as she watched them. She liked cows. She missed them.

She repeated the process with the second cow. Then, seizing the heavy buckets, she made her way back to the house.

As she came in the back door, Adam stumbled into the kitchen. The man looked wretched—dark circles under his eyes, his shirt wrinkled and untucked, his suspender straps dangling, his hair mussed up.

"Good morning," she whispered. "Is Lucas still asleep?"

"Ja." He stood, swaying, and knuckled his eyes. "It was a long night."

"So I gathered. Are you taking the day off from work?"

He glanced at the clock and she saw awareness creep into his eyes at the late hour. He groaned. "Overslept. So much to do…"

"I fed the chickens and milked the cows." She succeeded in keeping the smugness out of her voice as she hefted the full pails of milk onto the counter.

"You milked the cows?" He stared at the pails for a moment, then scrubbed a hand over his face. "Bless you, Ruth. I had no idea it was so late."

"If you like, I can walk over to the log yard and tell everyone you won't be at work today."

He gave a jerky nod. *"Ja*, please. Find Peter and tell him I'll be in around noon. I'll stay here with Lucas."

She left him to pull himself together, and hopped on the bicycle for the short ride to the log yard. She'd never been there, and was curious what it was like.

The fenced compound had stacks of logs, some raw, some peeled, and two homes in a partial state of construction. A crane stood idle, ready to move logs into position. She saw two men wearing hard hats, talking near one of the homes, and made her way to them.

"I'm looking for Peter," she said as she approached them.

One of the men smiled at her. "I'm Peter. May I help you?"

"I'm Ruth, the nanny to Adam's son, Lucas. I don't know if you heard, Lucas broke his arm yesterday at church." She paused as both men made noises of consternation. "Adam was up all night with him, and overslept. He wanted me to let you know he'll be in around noon or so."

"Oh, poor kid," exclaimed Peter. "Yes, that's fine. We wondered where he was. Tell him we'll keep working on the McKinney house." He gestured toward one of the unfinished cabins.

"I'll tell him. Thank you." She stared at the cabin a moment, curious how it was constructed, then rode the bicycle back toward the house.

When she entered the kitchen, both Adam and Lucas were sitting at the table, eating the biscuits and gravy she'd made earlier. Adam had an oversize mug of coffee at his elbow. His face had a scrubbed look, and his blue shirt was neatly tucked into his trousers, with the suspender straps properly sitting over his shoulders.

"Miss Ruth!" crowed Lucas, giving a small bounce in the chair. He, like his father, had dark circles under his eyes, but seemed in high spirits nonetheless.

"You're awake!" She crouched down and gave him a hug. "Your *dat* says you had a rough night, but I'm glad to see you up."

"*Dat* says Jacob's *mamm* can draw a picture on my cast. Can we go see her today?"

She chuckled at his enthusiasm. "Maybe. It depends."

Adam swallowed one of the biscuits she'd left tucked in a cloth-lined bowl. "*Danke*, Ruth, for doing all my chores this morning. And for making breakfast. And telling the men I'd be late. It was…quite a night."

"Has Lucas had his pain medication yet this morning?"

"Ja." Adam reached over and tousled his son's hair. "That's why he's feeling so frisky. I've already discovered that when the medication wears off, he knows it. I broke my ankle when I was about ten years old, so I remember the routine. It'll take about a week for the pain to fade."

"I've never broken a bone, so it's good you remember what it's like." Ruth saw that the morning's milk had already been strained and tucked away, and the steel bucket scrubbed clean and upended over the drain rack.

Adam glanced at the clock. "I'm actually feeling pretty *gut* myself. I know I'm not going to get a nap in, so I might as well get to work. *Vielen Dank* again for doing the barn chores this morning."

He drained his coffee, rose from the table and went into his small office to pull together whatever documents he needed for the day. He emerged, stuffing some papers into his leather portfolio. "I'm going to drop off the estimate you worked on with the new clients today," he told her. "I'll let you know what they say. Lucas, be *gut* for Miss Ruth, *ja*?" He leaned down and gave his son a kiss on the cheek.

Then he did something startling. While Lucas was distracted with his food, Adam caught her by the arm. "Ruth, *danke* again for everything…" Then he leaned in and kissed her.

She was caught entirely unprepared. If he'd meant for the kiss to be friendly and platonic, it backfired spectacularly. Instead, her eyes fluttered closed and the kiss lingered far beyond the boundaries of gratitude and into the realm of intimate.

Ruth had been kissed very few times in her life, more as an experiment than anything else. This was no experiment.

It ended sooner than she would have liked, which was probably a good thing. When he pulled away from her, his blue eyes looked dark.

Shaken, she leaned against the sink. "It won't work, Adam," she whispered. The unspoken reason hovered between them, as unbreachable as a wall.

"I know," he murmured. "A moment of madness. It won't happen again." He turned his back to her, and she saw his hands clench into fists. "I'm leaving now."

Through a window, she watched as he walked toward the log yard. Her hands trembling, she pressed a hand to her stomach and realized she actually had butterflies. Uh-oh. Not good.

Oblivious to the fireworks that had just taken place behind him, Lucas was nearly finished with his breakfast. Thankfully, the child had not broken his dominant arm, so he was able to eat with his right hand without a problem. Striving for normalcy, she sat down and reached for a biscuit. "I don't know if we'll have a chance to go see Jacob today, but when we do, I'm certain his mother would love to draw something on your cast. Do you want her to draw a dog, or something else?"

Distracting the boy with chitchat about pictures on the cast, she realized she was also diverting herself from thinking too much about the child's father.

Though it was a losing battle…

* * *

Adam hitched up Maggie the horse to the buggy and drove toward the log yard. He was angry with himself. Why had he kissed Ruth? He knew without a doubt that his spontaneous gesture had altered the situation between them. He blamed his sleep deprivation for the moment of weakness.

He warred with himself, battling the loyalty he felt for his late wife and his interest in the nanny who had come to his aid when he was in urgent need of help.

He rubbed his eyes, still gritty from his sleepless night caring for Lucas. He wondered if he should have taken the day off from work, but felt obligated to deliver the quote to the family across town who, he knew instinctively, would be excellent customers.

Peter, his foreman, walked out to meet him as Adam tied Maggie under a tree and unhitched her from the buggy until needed. "How's Lucas?" he asked.

"Recovering," Adam replied, and promptly yawned. "Sorry, I didn't get much sleep last night."

"That's what the nanny said. Tough on the poor kid, breaking his arm. And he's so active, too."

"It's *because* he's active that he broke his arm." Adam allowed himself a small smile. "The little monkey was climbing a tree after church, and fell."

A father of three himself, Peter chuckled. "Maybe it taught him a lesson."

"*Ja*, maybe." Adam patted Maggie's neck and followed the foreman into the log yard's office.

He sat at his desk while Peter reviewed the paperwork for the bid he had to present to the Johnsons. The numbers swam in front of his eyes. His mind wandered, recalling the scent of Ruth's hair...

"Boss?" Peter waved a hand before his face.

"Huh?" He squinted at Peter.

"I said, there's a problem right here." The foreman tapped a paper with a stubby finger and chuckled. "You *must* be tired."

"*Ja*, I am." Tired, and preoccupied with his son's nanny. Not good. He focused on Peter. "What kind of problem?"

"Here. You misquoted the base price of the logs. If the Johnsons signed off on this, we'd lose several thousand dollars."

Startled, Adam squinted at the numbers. His foreman was right. Ruth had pulled together the bid under his supervision, so this wasn't a mistake on her part. She had simply taken the numbers he'd provided her and worked up the bid.

He groaned. "I'm going to have to redo the whole thing since this base price is represented throughout."

"Do you have time?" Peter glanced at the clock.

"I'll make time." Annoyed at himself, Adam turned to a nearby file cabinet and snatched some blank bid forms.

It took an hour of intense calculation before the revised bid was ready. Adam hoped he hadn't made any more errors, but there was no time to double-check. If he was angry at himself before for that kiss, it was nothing next to his self-flagellation over his professional goof-up.

Finally, he gathered the papers together and shoved

them into his leather satchel, then went outside. Peter and his other men were trimming logs for another project. "I'm off to the Johnsons'," he called out to them. Peter waved a hand in acknowledgment.

Adam hitched Maggie back up to the buggy and headed through the gates of the log yard.

How could he have done that? How could he have taken one of the most important components of a bid—the base price of the logs used to assemble a structure—and provided Ruth with the wrong number?

Guiding Maggie toward town, he thought about the situation. What had possessed him to think he was qualified to run a business? He was a fine carpenter, no question, but it took more than carpentry skills to make a business succeed. It took business smarts, and that was something he apparently lacked. Peter was right. If the Johnsons had signed off on the bid, he would be legally bound to honor the contract, and his business would have lost a lot of money.

He automatically directed the horse toward the town's side streets to avoid the traffic on the main road. Should he close down the business? Should he go to work for someone else, simply to avoid having to deal with the business side of things? He marveled at Ruth's seemingly effortless facility with numbers. He couldn't impose on her more than he already was when it came to bids and estimates. The only solution—if he wanted to keep working for himself—was to hire an expert. He couldn't risk making another mistake like this.

He pulled up barely five minutes late to the Johnsons' building site, where the middle-aged couple waited next to their car. "Good afternoon!" he called, and decided to place the blame on Lucas rather than his own numerical incompetence. "I'm so sorry to be late. My son broke his arm yesterday, and I had a restless night with him. I overslept this morning and the day has gone downhill since." He gave them what he hoped was a rueful smile.

The couple made clucking noises of sympathy and assured him they weren't offended by his tardiness. As he spread out the paperwork and showed them the estimate for their cabin, he tried not to be distracted from the job at hand by thinking about either his own business woes or Ruth.

"This looks fine," Mr. Johnson assured Adam, after reviewing the paperwork. He glanced at his wife for approval. "We're very pleased with the plans and the cost. I have no problem signing off on the bid right now."

Adam was happy—and relieved beyond measure—at his response. By the time he headed back to work, it was late afternoon, and he had the signed estimate on the seat beside him in the buggy. This was the last job he would take before winter, and it reassured him that the business would remain solvent and he'd be able to pay his men through December. *"Danke, Gott,"* he whispered.

But there was still the issue with Ruth. He prayed he hadn't irrevocably damaged their working relationship.

He pulled into the log yard just as his men were getting ready to leave for the evening. He confirmed the new job with Peter, said good-night to everyone, and directed Maggie toward home.

He thought about what the bishop had said yesterday about him marrying Ruth. The church leader had basically given his blessing to Ruth, should she choose to become Amish—again.

Why would the bishop propose such a match? Suggesting someone who wasn't baptized—and didn't seem likely to become so—was highly unusual.

Ruth might have been born Amish, but she had been away from the church since she was eleven years old. Expecting she would return was unrealistic. Expecting she would return for the sole purpose of marrying him was hoping for the impossible.

Adam knew Amish converts were rare for a reason. And those that *did* convert usually didn't last. The one thing—the only thing—that would ensure such a conversion would be permanent was if it had a spiritual basis.

Ruth's spiritual life was none of his business. It was solely a matter between her and *Gott*. That was all. Bottom line, Ruth would have to convert because she felt led by *Gott* to join the church of her childhood. Once that decision was made, she would have to promise to put aside worldly things and abide by the rules of the *Ordnung*. She would have to live with the Amish for at least another year. She would have to take five months of classes prior to her baptism. And then, of course, he hoped she would be interested in marrying him.

It seemed like an impossible undertaking. He scowled at the scenery passing by him. The odds were certainly not in his favor.

And yet... Ruth didn't strike him as being overly interested in worldly fashions or conveniences. He had never seen her in anything but modest skirts and tops, and she didn't seem especially concerned that she had left her phone at that rest stop before he found her stranded on the side of the road. He knew many *Englischers* were devastated when they lost their phone, but she had just shrugged it off, and in fact seemed happy to be rid of it.

She was working in a home without electricity. And had taken it upon herself to do chores that were not part of her job description—cooking, cleaning, tidying—and didn't seem in the least bit fazed to tackle them without modern appliances. It was almost as if she had reverted to the muscle memory of her childhood.

And there seemed to be a definite spark between them. Adam tried not to dwell too much on that, but it was unmistakable.

Then there was Lucas. His *sohn* adored her. Ruth seemed to like Lucas as well.

In any other situation, Adam wouldn't hesitate to court the woman. But as it stood, there were insurmountable barriers between them.

He stabled the horse and went into the house. He found Lucas snuggled in Ruth's lap in a rocking chair, reading a story.

"Dat!" Lucas struggled to slide off her lap, then came over to hug his legs.

"There's my little man." Adam dropped his work satchel on the floor and squatted down to hug his child. "How do you feel? How's your arm?"

"Hurts." The boy smiled. "But Miss Ruth said tomorrow we can go see Jacob and ask his *mamm* to draw a picture on my cast."

"*Ach*, what a *gut* idea. She draws so nicely. Were you a *gut* boy for Miss Ruth today?"

"*Ja!*"

Adam smiled. Like his son would say anything else. He looked at Ruth for confirmation.

"Actually he was," she affirmed, putting the storybook aside and rising from the rocker. Her eyes met his briefly, then skittered away. "He took two naps, which isn't surprising considering the kind of night you must have had with him. I've given him pain medication twice. Once it kicks in, he seems to do all right. I need to go check dinner." She headed for the kitchen.

Adam rose and carefully swung Lucas into his arms. "Did I ever tell you the time I broke my ankle?" he asked the boy.

"*Nee!*" Lucas gazed at him with wide eyes.

"I was ten years old and playing soccer with some other boys. I kicked the ball and somehow missed it and kicked a tree instead. The tree kicked back and I broke my ankle." He chuckled. "You should have heard me howl! You were a lot braver than I was."

Holding Lucas, he followed Ruth into the kitchen where she was removing a quiche from the oven. He took a moment to savor the situation.

For years, ever since Bethany had died, he had come home to a patched-together household with the succession of *youngie* babysitters who watched Lucas but did little to make the house a *home*. But somehow, in an effortless way, Ruth had accomplished this. It wasn't just the housekeeping chores she did. It was the serene atmosphere she brought with her, an indefinable air that unified and knit everything together. No wonder Lucas was thriving.

He felt he needed to say something to Ruth, about his morning. But he felt tongue-tied. "Ruth, I…"

"I won't be eating dinner with you tonight," she interrupted. He saw her cheeks flare scarlet. "But I'll be here at the usual time tomorrow." She scurried away, and in a moment he saw her dash away on the bicycle.

Lucas was indignant at his nanny's rapid departure. "Why did she go?" he whined. "I want her to stay forever."

Adam soothed his son, distracting him with inquiries about his day, but he understood the boy's sentiment.

He wanted Ruth to stay forever, too.

Chapter Eleven

The next morning, Adam woke up feeling enormously refreshed. He'd slept through the whole night, a welcome change from the previous night's sleeplessness. Evidently Lucas had slept as well.

As he lay quietly, he thought about Ruth. She'd run away yesterday afternoon, clearly avoiding him. How would she behave today?

He heard some noises from his son's room. Adam catapulted out of bed, hoping the child was not in too much pain.

But it seems the boy had simply climbed out of bed to get a toy and then climbed back, where he was quietly playing. Adam stood in the doorway and smiled. "*Guder mariye*, little man. How are you feeling? How's your arm this morning?"

"*Oll recht.*" Lucas touched the cast. "I want Jacob's *mamm* to draw me a picture."

"Maybe Miss Ruth can bring you over there today. Are you ready to help me with chores?"

"Ja." He raised his arms to be lifted up.

Adam hoisted the child into his arms and kissed the boy's neck until he giggled. He loved the child more than any earthly thing. He'd never give up Lucas to another family for any reason. His *sohn* was a living legacy from Bethany.

"Let's get us both dressed, then you can help me feed the chickens," he told Lucas. "I think Mrs. Peachey is coming to get some milk today to make cheese, so you can watch me milk the cow, too."

"Can I squirt some milk at the cats?" Lucas wiggled in his arms.

"Ja, sure. They're getting the hang of things, aren't they? They're learning to catch what you aim at them."

Chattering, he helped Lucas into his everyday clothes, then got dressed himself.

"I think we need shoes this morning," he observed as they went into the kitchen. "It's starting to get chilly. Soon we'll have a frost, and we'll have to pull everything in from the garden before that happens." Adam sighed, thinking of the amount of autumn farm work competing with the amount of work from the log yard.

Work was a blessing, he reminded himself. It was better than the alternative, for sure and certain.

By the time Ruth pedaled up to the house on her bicycle, the barn chores were done and he had Lucas munching on a piece of toast with butter. He felt the familiar zing of happiness at seeing her parking the bike and walking up to the door.

"Miss Ruth! Miss Ruth!" squealed Lucas, bouncing in his seat.

"Stay here, I'll let her in," instructed Adam, striding toward the door.

She looked tired, as if she hadn't slept well. *"Guder mariye,"* he offered with a wary smile.

"Guder mariye," she returned. Her smile didn't quite reach her eyes. She slipped past him and went toward Lucas, focusing her attention on the child.

Adam sighed. It was his own fault Ruth was acting skittish. But how could he fix things? He wasn't at all sure.

Ruth watched Adam through the kitchen window as he walked to work. The awkwardness between them was palpable. Why did he have to go and kiss her yesterday? She couldn't stop thinking about it. She was annoyed at him for changing what had been a perfectly cordial working relationship into something different. Suddenly she was so acutely *aware* of him that it became awkward. She suspected he felt the same. Their easy camaraderie was gone. In its place were two people tiptoeing around each other.

She dropped into the kitchen chair opposite Lucas. "Did you sleep better last night?"

"Ja." Lucas touched his cast. "Can we go see Jacob's *mamm* today?"

Ruth chuckled. "You *really* want her to draw something on your cast, don't you? Okay, finish your breakfast and then let's pick some vegetables in the garden for a little while. We don't want to visit Jacob's *mamm too* early in the morning."

Around ten o'clock, with some fresh corn picked for

dinner and a few extra ears for Eva, Ruth took Lucas's hand and set out for the Hostetler home.

"Hello!" exclaimed Eva, when she opened the door. She leaned toward Lucas. "How's your arm, *liebling*? We were so worried about you."

"I'm *gut*." The boy lifted his cast. "Draw me a picture?"

Eva quirked a puzzled glance at Ruth.

"Lucas wanted to know if you could draw a picture on his cast," Ruth explained. "He's been talking about it constantly."

Eva squatted down beside Lucas. "What would you like me to draw?"

"A dog?" suggested Lucas.

The other woman chuckled. "Come into the kitchen. I'll get a piece of paper and draw something out. If you like it, then I'll draw it on your cast."

Eva's home, like Eva herself, was simple and welcoming. It was two stories high and large, since Ruth suspected Eva and her husband anticipated having many children to fill the empty bedrooms. As with most Amish homes, there were no pictures on the walls, and the furniture was plain and utilitarian. Pale green cotton curtains hung in the windows. But children's books and toys scattered about gave it a homey feel, with the morning sun streaming through the glass onto the golden floors and the braided rag rug.

It also was rather warm inside, since Eva was in the middle of canning green beans. Ruth walked into a kitchen of happy chaos, with baby Grace cooing in a bouncy seat in the middle of the table, and canning jars and chopped beans on the counters. Two large pressure canners dominated the propane stove, one over the heat and the other with the lid off.

Millie, Eva's six-year-old daughter, smiled as Ruth and Lucas came in. A miniature of her mother, the child was busy filling jars with cut beans using a wide-mouth funnel.

Eva found a pencil and a sheet of paper and sat down at the table. "So, what kind of dog do you want?" she asked.

"Like Buster," Lucas replied.

"And what do you want the dog to be doing?"

Lucas thought for a moment. "Chasing a cat up a tree?"

"Like this?" With a few deft strokes, Eva sketched a tree with a cat on a branch and a dog standing beneath, his paws on the trunk.

Watching this skill in action, Ruth blinked. "Wow," she breathed, amazed. "You're so talented. I had no idea you were such an artist."

Eva chuckled modestly. "Just a small gift from *Gott*," she said. "Lucas, if you like this, I'll draw it on your cast."

"Ja!" the boy agreed.

Eva found a felt-tipped marker. "I'll draw it so it's right side up for you," she told him. The children and Ruth gathered around as Eva tucked Lucas between her knees, rested his arm with the cast on the table, and translated the pencil sketch to the hard white material.

Within five minutes her sketch had come to life, complete with three-dimensional shadows created by little hatch marks. She added squiggles to indicate the dog's tail was wagging.

"How's that?" she said at last.

"I like it!" Lucas exclaimed. *"Danke!"*

Eva chuckled and released the child. *"Gut.* Now you and Jacob run along. There are cookies in the cookie jar if you want to bring some outside."

"Try not to jostle your arm," Ruth reminded the boy.

The children dashed outside. Ruth watched for a moment to make sure they weren't engaging in anything too strenuous. But they merely headed for a fort built at the base of a tree. She turned back toward Eva. "I had no idea you had an artist hidden inside you."

"I've always liked drawing," the other woman replied. "I never did anything with it, but it just seems to come naturally to me. Tea?"

"Yes, please."

Eva put a kettle of water on the stove next to one of the canners, and turned on the flame. "Sorry about the mess. Once the garden gets going, it's hard to keep up sometimes. Millie, *liebling,* if you want to go fill this basket with some more beans, Miss Ruth and I can cut them up while you play."

"Ja, Mamm." The child seized the basket and disappeared outdoors.

"And how's this little one doing?" Ruth wiggled the baby's tiny toes.

"She's a happy baby. You don't mind if I keep working, do you?"

"Of course not. Let me help."

The morning passed quickly as the women worked

on preserving food for the winter. Ruth enjoyed Eva's company.

"…and when Daniel learned he could get a farm for a quarter of the price of what it would have cost us in Indiana, that's how we ended up moving here," concluded Eva, relating the tale of her family's migration to Montana. "I miss the folks back home, of course, but it's so nice to have enough land to properly farm. Everything was getting so crowded back East."

Ruth snorted. "I came from New York City. You haven't seen *crowded* until you've been there."

"Do you like it here?"

"Yes." Ruth put aside a trimmed bean and picked up another. "I do. A lot. And it kind of surprises me."

She found herself giving the other woman an abbreviated version of life on Wall Street. "I guess you could say I thought I was successful," she concluded, dumping some cut beans into a bowl and reaching for another batch, "but I wasn't happy. I realize that now."

Eva chuckled. "I think a satisfied life is better than a successful life," she remarked. "I mean, you can't exactly claim preserving green beans is successful, but it's certainly satisfying—especially in midwinter, when you know your efforts are feeding your family long after the garden has gone dormant."

"True." Ruth was silent a moment, as she continued trimming. "I wonder what it would take for me to be satisfied?" she remarked after a while. "I wouldn't know where to start." Her thoughts flickered toward Adam and then jolted away.

"Hmm, I'm not sure." Eva looked thoughtful as she

filled jars with cut beans. "What are some recent moments where you've felt content and happy?"

"Church services," blurted Ruth, surprising herself. She paused a moment and realized it was true. "It brought back such memories. Happy memories."

"You should attend more, then. Speaking of which, would you like to help at the Stoltzfus farm before the next Sabbath? A bunch of women usually get together to help prepare it on the day before."

"Sure!" Ruth felt a blooming of warmth at the invitation. "What is it you do?"

"The Saturday before Church Sunday, everyone descends on the Stoltzfus farm and cleans it from top to bottom. The men do the outdoor work, the women do the indoor work."

"It actually sounds like fun."

"It is." Eva winked. "But just between you and me, I think the Stoltzfuses rather enjoy it, because it means the whole church pitches in to clean up their house and barn twice a month."

Ruth chuckled. "Smart. And how long does it take? All day?"

"*Nein*, only about an hour, maybe an hour and a half. There's usually a dozen each of men and women, and with so many people helping, it hardly takes any time. Adam usually comes with Lucas, and since quite a number of other families also bring their *kinder*, he'll have playmates."

"It sounds like it. Yes, I'd like to help. Is it a potluck? Should I bring anything?"

"*Nein*, because sometimes even a potluck can be a

burden on the host family. For that reason, make sure you eat before you get there."

"I will, thank you." A thought struck her, and she gave a rueful laugh.

"What's so funny?" Eva quirked an eyebrow.

"I was just thinking." Ruth smiled. "What would my coworkers or my boss say if they found me tucked in a small home in Montana canning beans and saying an Amish service was enjoyable? They simply wouldn't know what to make of it. If it wasn't about money, they usually weren't interested."

"I think that's the funny thing about success," Eva commented. "I would say if our success is measured by others, that's a problem. But satisfaction—well, that's measured by our own hearts and our own minds. Our own souls, too. That's what the Gospel teaches—what good is it for someone to gain the whole world if he loses his soul in the process?"

Ruth paused. That's what she had come so close to doing, wasn't it? She had gained the whole world—and nearly lost her soul in the process. The thought left her shaken.

Not for the first time, she wondered if God hadn't played a hand in the monumental financial blunder that had sent her fleeing across the country, the car trouble that had led her to be stranded on the roadside only to be rescued by Adam Chupp, and in Adam's job offer that had landed her in this kitchen, learning to can vegetables from a woman whose life was dedicated to humble service to her family and community. Ruth couldn't help but think Eva had found the secret of success *and* satisfaction.

"That's so true," she said slowly. "It—it frightens me to think that's what I was doing. I was working to gain the whole world and losing my soul in the process."

"I'm glad you're here," Eva said simply, with such sincerity that Ruth's eyes prickled. "I have no way of knowing how bad it was in your job, or what it was like for you, but you certainly seem happier and more content here."

"I am." Ruth spoke with conviction. "And that little one…" she nodded out the window where Lucas's laugh mingled with Jacob's "…is a joy. I spent so much time helping with younger foster siblings when I was a teenager, but none of them touched me as Lucas has."

"And what about Adam?"

Ruth froze at Eva's gentle question. She stared at her friend, hoping the warmth she felt on her cheeks wasn't coloring them pink. "What do you mean?"

"I mean, it's obvious he has feelings for you."

"But…but I'm not Amish."

"I know that. You know that. And believe me, he knows that. But sometimes the heart moves in a direction no one expects. Do you return his interest?"

"If I did, I wouldn't do anything about it." Ruth replied. "I remember enough of my Amish childhood to know that's a fast track to being shunned by the community. I wouldn't ever put him in that position."

"That's *gut* of you." Eva dropped canning lids into a pot of hot water to soften the gaskets. "Adam is a solid member of the church. But he's lonely. It took him a long time to get over his wife's passing. You're the first person he's looked at with any interest since then."

"Eva, what are you suggesting? That I become Amish so Adam and I could become a couple?"

The other woman shook her head. "Interest in a man is a very poor reason to come into the church. Those kinds of conversions don't last. Maybe what I'm doing is warning you, instead."

"Not to toy with his affections, you mean?"

"Something like that, *ja*."

"I'm not, believe me." That was why she had told him yesterday, after their kiss, that it wouldn't work. "But I'm not responsible for his feelings, either."

"Life is complicated, isn't it?" Eva gave her a lopsided smile.

"Yes. But not nearly as complicated as what I left behind. I've…I've come to put more trust in God, something I haven't thought about doing in a long time."

"It's all in *Gott*'s hands," agreed Eva. "Here, I think the jars are ready to put in the canner."

Ruth began tidying the table as Eva stacked jars in the canner, trying not to think how much she wanted to do just what Eva warned her against—toy with Adam's affections.

After his play date with Jacob, Lucas was exhausted. Plus, Ruth could tell his arm hurt. "Let's give you some medicine, then it's time for a nap," she told the boy.

"Story?"

"Of course. But medicine first."

The child obligingly took the pain medication, then

Ruth tucked him into bed, took one of his favorite books, and read to him. It took only a few minutes for his eyes to close and his breathing to deepen.

She looked down at his innocent little face, with the curly blond hair that had a tendency to fall over his eyes. What a beautiful child.

She had never considered herself overly maternal before, but something about Lucas brought those instincts out in her. What would it be like to have a child of her own?

Restless, she rose from the chair beside Lucas's bed and wandered the quiet house. It was her afternoon habit during the boy's naptime to tidy the house and plan something for dinner. Since they'd spent most of the morning at Eva's, there was hardly anything to do as far as cleaning up.

She picked up a stray toy on the floor near the small room Adam used as a home office. Holding the stuffed bear, she lingered in the doorway. Then, curious, she went inside. While Adam had never gone so far as to indicate his office was off-limits, she knew she had no business being in there.

But she was interested in how he did things. He already knew carpentry, he'd said, but only learned how to build log homes when he came out to Montana working for the larger company. It was for Lucas's sake he'd started his own business, something that would allow him to stay close to home to raise his son. While it was a sentiment Ruth admired, she wondered just how qualified Adam truly was to handle the financial side of things. After all, he had admitted to her that he wasn't good with numbers.

Ruth put down the stuffed bear and shamelessly started rifling through paperwork. Receipts, expenses, payouts, sketched-out floor plans, log purchases…it was all there. And it was all disorganized.

The four-drawer file cabinet against one wall wasn't much better. She went through the random folders, none of which were properly labeled. How did he get anything done? How did he plan to expand the business if he couldn't find anything? She twitched with the urge to straighten out his business affairs.

But as she looked through things that were none of her business, she started forming an overall picture of a man in over his head.

What she saw confirmed her theory that Adam simply wasn't easy with numbers. He was clearly a brilliant carpenter, but no good when it came to business matters. All her financial training surged to the forefront as she nosed through his paperwork. He'd done a lot to get his business off the ground, but he could do so much more! It would help to get organized, yes. But more importantly, he looked like he needed help with the Big Picture.

Her years on Wall Street had taught her that the Big Picture was extremely important. Growth was supreme. There were advertising venues he could utilize, bookkeeping methods he could apply, and marketing options he could look into. Revenue streams, return on investments, five-year plans, ten-year plans…all those techniques could get Adam's start-up business on course for long-term viability and keep him working for decades.

Her mind buzzed with the possibilities. Adam had said his one condition was that he'd never be away from home on account of Lucas. Well, okay then. What about ramping up his business from home? He could offer set floor plans rather than drawing up custom plans from scratch. He could offer subcontracting services, hiring out the necessary tasks of installing the foundation, plumbing and wiring, rather than leaving that aspect up to customers. He could even franchise. He could…

He could be rich if he wanted.

Okay, maybe not rich, but certainly better off.

She picked up the stuffed bear and retreated from the office, making sure nothing was disheveled. Maybe she shouldn't have snuck in and snooped through all his paperwork. But it certainly gave her a clearer picture of the uphill battle he faced. No wonder he had moments of anxiety and wondered if he'd be able to support his son without having to go back to work for someone else.

If that was his goal—to keep the business running— then she could help. She knew she could. She had a double degree in business and finance. She had several years of working on Wall Street. She had…

She had a spectacular investment failure under her belt. "That's how you ended up in Montana, remember?" she berated herself.

Putting the stuffed bear in the open crate of toys, Ruth went into the kitchen and began assembling a casserole for dinner. Yes, she had fled from a bad job of causing a lot of people to lose money. It was how she'd lost all her own money, something she was still too humiliated to confess to her foster parents. But that didn't mean her education and her experience were useless. Business was still business, after all.

By the time Lucas woke up from this nap, the casserole was assembled and resting in the icebox.

"How's your arm?" she inquired as she snuggled the child in the rocking chair, letting him come out of his sleep daze slowly.

"Okay," he said. "I like the dog." He touched the drawing Eva had made on his cast. "It's pretty."

"Jacob's mother draws so well," she agreed. "No wonder you wanted her to be the one to make the picture. Hey, what do you say we go gather some eggs from the chicken coop?"

Lucas nodded, but the child seemed inclined to stay where he was, and Ruth rested her cheek on top of his hair and silently rocked for a few more minutes.

She knew Lucas was starting to look at her as a mother figure. It was an occupational hazard she hadn't considered—that while she was taking care of a motherless child, the child might seek a mother. What would happen to Lucas after she left?

Left for where?

Rocking the boy, Ruth allowed her mind to explore the unknown and, frankly, scary future after this job ran its course. Yes, she could probably return to New York. She might even be able to sweet-talk her way back into a job with her old company.

But did she want that?

She rested her head on the back of the rocking chair

and looked out the window. Rather than dense skyscrapers and hordes of people moving around, she saw fields of harvested wheat and dark pine forests. Rather than the din of endless traffic and urban bustle, she heard meadowlarks and robins singing. Even in town, she saw people with smiles rather than the irritation that seemed to come with life in a huge city. Could she give this up?

For the first time in a long time, she thought about the cell phone she'd left behind at that rest stop so far away. What amazed her was how little she cared about it. Accidentally losing it was freeing. In fact, just thinking about her phone made her tense up.

She had a moment's unease. Was it God's hand that had caused her to leave it behind? Was He trying to tell her something? Was her carelessness actually a divine message?

She had some thinking to do. And, perhaps, an offer to make to Adam.

Chapter Twelve

Waiting in line late on Friday afternoon at the post office, Adam shuffled forward with glacial speed. The small-town post office rarely had more than one window open, and someone ahead of him was mailing a lot of packages all at once. Adam shrugged. He needed stamps, and this was the place to get them.

No one commented on his straw hat or suspenders, for which he was grateful. The town of Pierce had accepted its Amish residents and no longer felt the need to pepper every church member with questions. Many businesses had even installed hitching posts for horses, which made things considerably more convenient. Maggie was tied to one right now, patiently waiting.

He flipped through the letters and bills he was mailing. Two letters to two of his siblings back in Indiana. A letter to his old bishop. Three bills.

Sighing, he glanced around for something distracting. Next to him was a standing table that held a variety of domestic and international address forms and other standard materials for a post office. Over the table was a cork bulletin board. Absently, he studied the flyers and notices pinned to the board. A lost dog. An announcement for an upcoming event in the town's park. A yard sale. An offering for pet-sitting services. A missing person flyer.

Adam did a double take and stared. The missing person flyer had a photo that looked familiar. His heart started thudding in alarm even as his mind tried to deny the obvious.

"Have you seen this woman?" shouted the flyer in large-type font. Beneath the banner headline was a photo of Ruth.

She was wearing business attire with well-coiffed hair and careful makeup, clearly a photo used for employment applications or other professional purposes. Eyes wide, he read the material beneath.

The information said Ruth had disappeared in late August from both her job and her apartment in New York City. She was last seen in a dark blue Jeep Liberty. There was reason to believe she was somewhere in Montana.

He felt cold prickles down his spine. The dark blue vehicle was what she'd been driving when he found her stranded. She'd said she had left a job in New York City. But she had always been cagey about her reasons for hitting the road and wandering the country. She was equally evasive about letting her foster parents know of her whereabouts.

And now here was her photo on a flyer in a post office. The air of mystery she always wore now hit him.

Had Ruth broken the law? Had he entrusted his son to the care of a fugitive?

But the flyer didn't indicate she was *wanted*, only *missing*.

Glancing ahead at the line of people waiting patiently, he saw no one was watching. He reached over, slipped the thumbtack from the flyer, folded up the paper and tucked it in his pocket.

Ruth had some explaining to do.

It was hard to keep his mind focused after that. He resisted the urge to unfold the flyer and stare at it. Finally, he was able to purchase his stamps and mail his letters. He finished a few other errands—hardware store, building supply store—then directed his horse and buggy back home through an autumn landscape that was at the peak of its beauty, with wild plum and apple, hawthorn and aspen contrasting with the dark green of the region's dominant coniferous forests.

But his mind buzzed with worry. Why was Ruth missing? Why was there a flyer looking for her?

He pulled the buggy around to the barn and unhitched the horse. Lucas came running out of the house. *"Dat!"*

"There's my little man!" He picked up the boy and gave him a hug. "How does your arm feel? Better?"

"Ja. Miss Ruth, she played hide-and-seek with me today because she said it was a good game to play that wouldn't hurt my arm. And see? She drew a picture on it, too." The child pointed to a clumsy rendition of a chicken on his cast.

"Well, let me get the animals done for the night and

we'll go inside." With the boy at his heels, Adam stabled the horse, made sure Maggie had food and water, and gave her a quick brushing. He fed and watered the cows and chickens, then took Lucas's hand and headed for the house.

The smell of dinner reached him when he was still outside. That was something he had come to appreciate. Rather than coming back from work to a house with a discontent child and domestic chores to complete before nightfall, these days he came home to a warm and welcoming scene: a meal on the table, a happy son, everything tidy. And it was all thanks to Ruth.

"Gut'n owed," she greeted him, smiling.

"Gut'n owed," he returned, removing his hat and hanging it on a peg by the door. He noted she had been making a conscious effort to speak more *Deutsch.* To practice, she said.

She wore a skirt and blouse he had seen before, her wardrobe being rather limited. She had a smear of flour on her cheek, which emphasized the luminous brown of her eyes. She moved easily around the kitchen—stirring something on the stove, setting a basket of warmed rolls on the table, placing a dish in the sink. She didn't look like a woman who'd committed a crime. So why was she missing? What was she running from? What had she fled? So many questions were floating around in his head.

She set the table while he washed up at the sink. She asked him about his day, as a wife might do. He told her a few anecdotes of his work, as a husband might do. Meanwhile the folded-up flyer burned a hole in his pocket.

He planned to ask her for an explanation before she left for the night. He needed to know more about the woman he had hired to care for his son.

He sat down for the meal. Said a silent blessing. Made polite chitchat while eating. Then after dinner, when Lucas was distracted by his toys in the living room, Adam spoke. "Ruth, I need to show you something."

"Yes?" She stood up as if to start clearing the table.

"This." He removed the paper from his pocket, unfolded it and handed it to her.

She took the paper. Her eyes widened and her face went pale. She dropped bonelessly back in the kitchen chair, staring.

"I want an explanation," he said, point-blank. He didn't care if his tone sounded harsh. "Why did you leave your job in New York City? And I need a truthful answer this time."

She looked at him silently, almost fearfully. At her deer-in-the-headlights expression, he added in a quieter voice. "Have you committed a crime?"

She jerked. "No!"

"Then why is there a flyer being posted in the local post office that you're missing? You're watching my son. I have a right to know."

She heaved an enormous sigh. "If you must know, I'm running away from humiliation."

Whatever Adam expected, it wasn't this. He frowned. "From *humiliation*? I found you stranded after what you admitted was a purposeless cross-country trip. It must have been quite a humiliation if you left everything behind, told no one where you were going, and refused to get in contact with your foster parents."

She met his eyes unflinchingly. "It was."

He kept his voice inflexible. "Ruth, I need to hear the story." It was more than just his concerns over who was watching his son. He also needed to know more about her background before he could be sure she was a woman worth guiding toward his faith. He had to decide if she was a woman worth courting.

Deep down, Ruth had known the day of reckoning would come. In some ways it was a relief to get her burden off her chest.

She scrubbed a hand over her face. "It's a long story," she said. "Are you sure you want to hear all of it?"

"*Ja*. All of it." He leaned back in his chair.

"Okay." She toyed with a fork. "I told you how I was raised by foster parents after my own parents were killed. They are good people. But the one thing they always emphasized was independence. What I mean by that is, they encouraged all the older teens in their care to develop a skill or career that would allow them to live independently. Some of my foster siblings couldn't, of course. They had some physical or mental challenges. But for those of us who could, the goal above all else was the ability to earn a living."

Adam nodded. "Makes sense."

"Yes, it does. I was always good with math and numbers, so my foster father suggested I go into business

and finance. It wasn't a field I was especially passion-
ate about, but I did well in school and managed to land
some entry-level jobs on Wall Street after graduation."
She paused, trying to marshal her thoughts.

"And then…?" prompted Adam.

"And then—I started advancing on Wall Street," she
continued. "I learned I had a flair for investment and
making businesses grow. My responsibilities increased.
My bank balance increased. My foster father was proud
of me. He told me I would be wealthy in no time if I
kept up the good work. I became focused on money, on
wealth. And it—it changed me."

Adam's forehead wrinkled. "Changed you in what
way?"

Her hand clenched the fork. "I became…well, arrogant. Overly confident in my abilities. In short, I
thought I was a big shot, I admired the easy way those
above me in the company advised their clients on how
to invest. More often than not, that advice paid off and
the clients made money. And so did my bosses. And so
did the company. Money was everywhere."

Adam's forehead furrowed. "Money was everywhere?
What does that mean?"

"Money was all people talked about." She slowly
unclenched her hand from the utensil and laid it on
the table. "How to make it, how not to lose it. Oddly,
money itself was the focus, not what could be done with
it. No one talked about buying yachts or taking round-
the-world luxury tours with it, though I'm sure people
did those things. Instead, making money was a passion.
A means unto itself."

"That doesn't sound healthy."

"It's not. Believe me, it's not. And the hours we junior investors put in were insane. It wasn't just the hours. It was the lack of control of those hours. Our lives didn't belong to us, they belonged to the company. We were taught unflagging loyalty early on, and that loyalty precluded everything else—our families, our health, our recreation. Everything."

He shook his head. "So why did you stay?"

She met his eyes. "Because it was addictive. It became a game, to see how much money I could earn, and how fast. Besides, it was rather heady for a young professional to be making my mark in the finance world. My foster parents were so proud of me. They said I was the most successful of all the foster kids they'd ever raised."

She continued. "Those of us who were junior analysts called it the 'Wall Street education.' We could not question things or we'd risk losing our jobs. It was like a two-year trial by fire that encompassed every aspect of our lives."

"I would have hated that," Adam noted.

She pushed the fork around the plate. "Yes. As I said, it just kinds of pulls you in. Wall Street changed me. It changed all the junior analysts. I became sharper, more direct when talking to my foster parents. How could they possibly understand the intricacies and pitfalls of my new life?" She shook her head. "Deep down I knew I was wrong, but I was so immersed in the culture that I couldn't pull back."

"And this happened to everyone?"

"Yes. If it didn't, you left. A couple of junior analysts cracked under the strain and left, and the rest of us looked at them with pity. I mean, they're the ones who recaptured a real life, yet we thought they couldn't handle 'real life.'"

"It sounds very unbalanced."

"Oh, it is. Friends and family—any social life whatsoever—became less important. Life inside Wall Street becomes all-consuming, and everything else is dismissed as a distraction."

"Including…" Adam paused. "Including faith?"

"Absolutely." She spoke without hesitation. "It got to the point where all any of us wanted was money."

"And did they pay you well?" asked Adam.

"Yes. I had enough of a frugal background to not overspend. I wasn't rich, of course—at least by Wall Street standards—but I was making it in New York. I didn't own much because apartments in New York are so tiny, and besides I never spent any time there. Almost everything I owned, except for a couple pieces of furniture, I was able to pack into my car when I left."

Adam waved a hand. "I'll admit, this story is interesting. Horrifying, yes. But fascinating." He shook his head. "Why didn't you leave?"

"Because I was a woman making it in a male-dominated field, and I was proud of myself. Proud of my accomplishments. And then—it all came crashing down."

"How?"

"I overheard a short snippet of my boss on the phone with someone, talking about a hot investment. I looked into it—briefly—and thought he was right. It was the 'briefly' that was my undoing. It seemed like too good a deal to miss out on. I advised my client base to invest, and I foolishly took every last penny of my own savings and invested it, too. Within days I lost it all. My clients' investments were wiped out, and they were furious. My boss was furious. I had about three thousand dollars left in my checking account after that disastrous investment, and that was all I had left to show for my two years on Wall Street. As it turns out, the part I *didn't* hear when my boss was on the phone was that the investment was too risky, too volatile."

Adam winced. "Ouch."

"Yes. So I went back to my apartment, packed my bags, cleaned out the place and left. I couldn't bear to tell my foster parents what I had done. I couldn't stand the thought of facing the consequences of my actions. I just got in my car and started driving. I stopped the next day in some little town in New Jersey, withdrew the money from my checking account and closed the account. Then I just…drove."

"With no destination."

"Right. I'd stop when I was too exhausted to drive and check into whatever motel I came across. I turned my phone off—I didn't want to see the texts or hear the rings as people attempted to reach me. I just drove."

"What did you hope to do by just driving?" Adam looked honestly baffled.

"I—I can't even begin to tell you how I felt. I was numb at first, just too numb to think. Then I was ashamed. Not just for losing everyone's money, but because I had drifted so far away from the person I thought I should be." Tears welled up. "And I was far too ashamed to call my foster parents and tell them what happened. I was their golden girl, and I'd messed up."

"Do you think they're the ones who put out this alert?" Adam tapped the flyer.

"Possibly. I don't know. Maybe." She fished a hand-kerchief from her pocket and mopped her eyes just as Lucas came back into the kitchen. The child took one look at her and climbed into her lap.

And then she started to cry.

Chapter Thirteen

Ruth rode her bike home that evening, feeling drained.

She hardly noticed the scenery around her—the open valley in which the Amish settlement was situated. The foothills of dark conifers. The Bitterroot Mountain range to the west. The dry grasses alongside the gravel road, waiting for the late autumn rains to start.

Instead, confessing her transgressions to Adam caused her to relive the emotions she'd felt as she wandered the country after fleeing New York. She barely remembered how she'd gotten through those first few days.

Then, when Lucas climbed into her lap half an hour ago, the tears had finally come, the understanding that she had lost a little part of her humanity. But she'd wept because of a great realization: working for Adam, caring for Lucas, she had gained that humanity back again.

It was odd how fulfilling she found her current job to be. There were none of the perks she had in her last job, but neither was there stress. Ruth actually stopped her bicycle by the side of the road, lifted her head and took a deep breath of the cool mountain air.

The stress was the most insidious thing of all in her last job. The adrenaline coursing through her system on a daily basis had taken a toll on her health, but it was gone now. Instead she commuted by bicycle and spent her working hours watching a rambunctious little child whose very boyishness made her feel alive and needed. And wanted.

She frowned at a distant tree where a hawk was perched. And what about Adam? Did he play a part in her future?

She didn't know.

But he was right in one regard. He'd told her she needed to get in touch with her foster parents, who were doubtless frantic with worry about her absence.

She remounted the bicycle and headed for town. For too long she had made the excuse that her foster parents couldn't spare the energy to worry about her since she was just one of a long assembly line of children they cared for.

But that was wrong. She owed a debt of gratitude to the couple who had taken her in when she was at her most vulnerable. They had done their best by her. They had launched her into a career she'd seemed well suited for. It certainly wasn't their fault she'd messed up.

But oh, having to confess she'd lost all her money… that was the worst.

Back at the boardinghouse, she parked the bicycle in the shed and made her way indoors. For once she hoped to avoid Anna Miller and her interest in the day's doings. Instead she simply wanted to get to her room and tackle the dreaded task of calling her foster parents.

She was in luck. There were some guests checking in—an older couple who looked like they were passing through town on a leisurely trip. Ruth merely greeted Anna in passing and climbed the stairs without issue.

She entered her room and closed the door behind her, eyeing the telephone on the bedside table. She had never even lifted the receiver in the entire time she'd lived here, except to talk to the mechanic when her car was declared unfixable. In fact, there was dust on it. She wiped it off, picked up the receiver and called home.

Her foster mother, Pam, answered with a distracted air. "Hello?" In the background, Ruth could hear the usual clamor of multiple children.

"Hi, Mom," she said. "It's Ruth."

"Ruth? Ruth!" The woman's voice rose almost to a scream. "Dave, Ruth is on the phone! Oh, honey, we've been so worried. Are you okay?"

A click indicated her foster father had picked up another line. "Ruth! Where are you, baby? Do you need any help?"

"I'm fine. I'm working in Montana. I—I owe you both such an apology. I didn't call earlier because I was so embarrassed about what happened in New York."

"We got the police involved," said Dave. "No one knew what happened to you. You left your apartment, cleaned out your bank account and disappeared. It wasn't until someone turned in your phone somewhere in Montana that we had a clue where you might be. We feared the worst."

Ruth pressed a hand to her forehead in remorse. "I can't believe I put you through all that. It seems like a nightmare now, a distant nightmare."

She told her foster parents all about her woes, and finally confessed she'd lost all the money she'd saved, by taking her own bad investment advice.

"All the financial independence you tried to teach me—I went and ruined it," she said in a voice thick with tears. "It was just too humiliating to admit what I'd done, so I packed my car with everything I could transport and just hit the road."

"Oh, Ruth." Her foster mother's voice was choked. "Everyone makes mistakes." She sniffed. "So where are you now?"

"In a little town in western Montana called Pierce," Ruth replied. "It's kind of funny how I ended up here. After I left New York, I zigzagged this way and that, trying to figure out what to do. I found myself stranded outside this town after I accidentally left my phone at a rest stop a hundred miles away. A man rescued me, then later hired me to watch his little son. He's Amish, believe it or not. I didn't know there was an Amish settlement in Montana, but there is. I just happened to stumble upon the only Amish community in the state. What are the odds?"

"Ruth, you need to know something," interrupted David, her foster father. "Your company on Wall Street has been trying to get hold of you. It seems your boss was up to no good, deliberately leading people into bad investments while pocketing kickbacks. While you were wrong to advise clients without proper research, what your boss was doing was highly illegal. Apparently you've been exonerated for any culpability about the investment losses, and I was told you could even have your old job back if you want to."

Ruth jerked upright. "You're kidding."

"I'm not," David replied. "So you can go back to Wall Street, if you want to."

Remembering her old boss and his obsession with money, at some level Ruth wasn't surprised by the news.

"No," she said slowly. "No, I don't want to go back to Wall Street."

"Do you need any money?" David asked, ever practical.

"No, I'm fine," she replied. "I'm working as a nanny, watching a little boy. The family is Amish and the father is a widower. My original goal was to work here just long enough to buy another car, but now...now I'm not sure about that. It's a nice little town, similar to what I remember when I was growing up. And the little boy I'm watching, he's a darling. To be honest, I'm not looking forward to going back to New York and immersing myself again in the same kind of stressful environment as before."

"Do what you need to do," her foster father advised. "If you didn't like your job in New York, don't go back, especially if you're happy with what you're doing now."

"I was just so embarrassed to admit I lost all my savings," she admitted. "I thought you'd be so disappointed in me."

There was a slight pause, and then her foster father said, "Let me tell you a little secret, kiddo. One of the reasons I've always focused on financial stability among our kids is because I, too, made a stupid error when I was a young man. Lost all my savings. It was a blow, let me tell you."

Ruth sank back down on the bed, a smile twitching her lips. "You never told me that, Dad!"

"Too embarrassed," the older man admitted. "And I don't want to go into any more detail because it's *still* embarrassing." She heard a rueful smile in his tone of voice. "But you did everything else right—you avoided credit card debt, you lived frugally. You're young enough that you'll be able to overcome this and recoup your losses. So don't give up."

"Honey, our goal was always to get you launched into successful adulthood," Pam said gently. "You always seemed to be doing so well on Wall Street. We had no idea it was as bad as all that."

Ruth's eyes prickled. "I didn't want to admit I wasn't cut out for that kind of lifestyle," she confessed. "Maybe it's not bad for some people, but until I left I didn't realize how wrong it was for me. I've been so much happier here."

"Must be that Amish upbringing," David chuckled. "It sounds like it's coming back to you."

"Yeah, I guess it is," she replied in some surprise. She hadn't really stopped to think about it. "Anyway, since I don't have a phone anymore, you can reach me at this little boardinghouse house I'm staying at." She gave them the phone number and address.

She spent a few more minutes on the phone with them, catching up on the details of their lives, some of her foster siblings and the new children they had taken in.

"Stay in touch, dear," advised Pam as the conversation concluded.

"I will. If I decide to move on, I'll let you know. But for now, I'll be here."

They all said goodbye and hung up. Then Ruth lay back on the bed and stared at the ceiling. There was so much to admire about Pam and David. Ruth was glad she had called her foster parents. She felt more at peace now than she had felt in ages.

But the question still remained, what about her future? She had told Adam she would stay on the job until his rush of projects was completed. But did she want to move on after that? She could buy a car and hit the road, but then what?

For the first time in a long time, she thought hard, practical thoughts about her future. As Pam had said, their goal was to launch her into successful adulthood. But what defined success? She felt more fulfilled taking care of Lucas than she ever had working twenty-hour days on Wall Street. Was that success? Her colleagues might disagree.

But staying here in Pierce—she liked the idea, at least for the time being. She wondered if Adam would want her to watch Lucas even after his busy season ended.

And would he continue to want to see her? And that, more than almost anything else, was an intriguing thought.

She thought about what her foster father had said.

She was young enough to recoup her losses. But what did she lose by leaving her high-pressure Wall Street job? Nothing except money. What did she gain?

The whole world.

Chapter Fourteen

When Ruth arrived at the farm the next morning, Adam saw she looked tired but more peaceful.

"You talked to your foster parents?" he guessed.

"Yes." She reached down and swung Lucas into her arms as the child catapulted out of the kitchen toward her. She gave the boy a smacking kiss on the cheek. "We talked for at least an hour," she told him. "They're such good people. They fully understood why I left New York. But they told me something interesting, too. Apparently my boss is in hot water for bad investment advice and getting kickbacks. The so-called 'investment advice' I overheard was part of that scam. One of the reasons they were looking for me is because my dad said I was completely exonerated and could have my old job back if I wanted it."

Adam tensed and went still. "And would you want to?"

She met his eyes. "No."

Relief flooded his system. "I'm glad," he said simply.

She bounced Lucas in her arms. "How could I give up watching this little man, anyway? Oof, down you go, Lucas. You're heavy."

"And I need to get going." Adam glanced at the clock. "The men will be arriving at the log yard, and I need to unlock the gates."

As he walked toward the log yard, he considered Ruth's decision to not return to her old job. She seemed firm. But what would happen when his busy season ended and he no longer needed her to watch Lucas? What then? Would she stay in Pierce? Get another job somewhere else?

He knew one thing: he didn't want her to go. But he didn't know how to convince her to stay, either.

The matter plagued him all day. As he debarked logs and notched corners, he mulled it over and was no closer to an answer.

At the end of the day, he walked home, back into the atmosphere of domestic tranquility he never failed to appreciate.

"Dat!" Lucas ran toward him.

"There's my boy!" Adam lifted the child into his arms. "Were you a *gut* boy for Miss Ruth today?"

"Ja!"

"And how's your arm feeling?"

"Oll recht. Miss Ruth makes it better."

Ruth smiled at the boy's innocent explanation. "I think he means the pain medication makes it better," she explained with a smile.

Adam put Lucas back down and sniffed the air. "Dinner smells *gut."*

"And it's just about ready." She lifted Lucas's booster seat into place and turned to take the casserole out of the oven.

Before she got that far, a crunching sound made her snap upright and stare at Adam. It sounded like car wheels on gravel. "What's that?"

Adam strode into the living room and looked out the front window. "Someone's here," he remarked in surprise. "Someone just drove up."

"In a car?"

"Ja." He jammed his hat back on and went outside.

The Amish settlement seldom saw motorized vehicles, with the exception of the trucks that came into the log yard. The idea of a car driving up instead of a buggy was so novel that Lucas dashed over to the front window to see.

Adam strode out of the house and up the front walkway, where Buster was at the fence line, barking and wagging his tail.

A middle-aged couple emerged from an expensive late-model sedan. The woman was attractive and stylishly attired in suede boots, black wool slacks and a deep purple cashmere sweater. "Oh, look at this cabin!" she cooed. "Isn't it darling!" She began taking photos with her cell phone.

Adam stiffened. As the dog continued to bark and demand attention, he turned and called, "Ruth, please bring Buster inside." The screen door opened and the dog disappeared.

The man, who was handsome with silver hair,

walked around the vehicle toward the gate. "Are you Adam Chupp?" He had a deep, booming voice.

"I am, *ja*." Adam said curtly.

The visitor extended a meaty hand. "I'm Robert Tresedor. Nice to meet you. I understand you're the one to talk to about building a log cabin for us."

Adam shook hands but remained unsmiling as the woman continued to take photos of the house, the yard and himself. "I have a business making kit cabins," he confirmed, then winced as the woman held up her phone right in front of him and took a picture. "Ma'am, please don't do that."

"Oh. Sorry." She grinned and put her phone down. "It's just that you look so quaint, all dressed up!"

Adam had met many tourists in Indiana who seemed to think the Amish were part of a movie set, attired in the clothing of film extras. But he had seldom met anyone as bold and disrespectful as this woman.

"So here's the deal." To Adam's astonishment, the man opened the yard gate and came straight through into the yard uninvited, trailed by the woman. "My wife, Alice, and I are thinking of moving to this area. I'm retiring, you know, after a successful career as an attorney. We have a nice little place in Los Angeles with another house in Billings, but the wife and I are interested in escaping the big city. A friend suggested we look at Pierce."

Meanwhile his wife, Alice, traipsed through the yard photographing flowers and the cabin, and even made her way around the side and started examining the garden and chicken coop. Adam prayed Ruth and Lucas would stay indoors.

"So Alice would have a log cabin as our country home," continued Robert benevolently. "Always make the wife happy, that's my motto. So when I heard you do cabins, I wanted to come talk to you right away about the design we have in mind."

From the corner of his eye, Adam saw Alice disappear behind the house and wondered what she was doing. "I'm sorry, but I'm booked solid through fall, and most building stops during the winter here, when there's snow on the ground."

"Not a problem, not a problem," the man rumbled. "If we find property we like, we wouldn't be ready to break ground until spring anyway. This way, too, we can book your exclusive services in advance." The man chuckled. "Once the project starts, we don't want any distractions on your part!"

"I'm sorry, but that won't work." Adam strove to keep his voice pleasant. "I have a wide customer base and can't take on any exclusive projects. However, I can recommend another builder who might be able to help you."

The man's bonhomie disappeared and his voice became gruff. "But I want you. I've heard you're the best."

"I appreciate the endorsement, but I don't think I'm the right man for the job. There are several other cabin builders in the region. I'm sure any one of them would be more than happy to tackle your project."

"I can pay you well." The man's bushy eyebrows

waggled suggestively. "Very well. Well enough to engage your services exclusively."

"I'm sorry, but no."

Tresedor scowled. "You're being unreasonable."

"On the contrary, I'm simply making you aware of my limitations. I'm a small builder and can only take on a limited number of projects. That's why I suggest you use a larger company. They would certainly have the resources to accommodate you."

Tresedor crossed his arms on his broad chest. "I can make this difficult for you," he warned. "I have a lot of influence and can let others know you're refusing to work for me. That won't reflect well on your business's future."

"You're free to do as you wish," Adam replied tightly, "but I fail to see how recommending you to a more qualified builder is not in your best interest."

The man harrumphed in annoyance, then looked over as his wife emerged from the other side of the house. The woman looked pleased with herself as she continued photographing every aspect of the property.

"Darling, this man is refusing our business," Tresedor informed her.

The woman's smile was wiped off her face as she walked back toward the gate. "What?!"

"I'm simply informing your husband that I'm not the best man for the job," Adam told her. "Your project sounds very complicated, and I'm too small a business to do it properly."

She scowled with an expression remarkably similar

to her husband's. "After all this effort, you can't turn us down!"

It was all Adam could do to keep from shaking his head in dismay and amazement. "There are three excellent log home companies in Missoula alone, and I know of several more in Butte and Great Falls. They're all highly recommended, have much larger staffs, and teams of builders who I'm sure can handle exclusive projects such as yours without a problem."

"How dare you!" The woman's face flushed red with anger. Suddenly her face was no longer as attractive.

Adam raised his eyebrows. "I'm trying to find you the best match for your needs," he replied, keeping his voice calm. "Why would you want to use a business that's too small to give you the best service?"

"You'll be hearing from us!" the woman growled. "No one tells us no when we want something."

Adam almost laughed, but managed to stifle the impulse. "I'm always glad to hear from people," he said. "I look forward to hearing how one of the other businesses can make your dream home a reality. Good afternoon." He turned and walked toward the house.

He could hear angry muttering from behind him, but he didn't look back. As he entered the house, he heard a car door slam. The vehicle's engine revved, and tires spun on the gravel as the car sped off.

He closed the door behind him and whooshed out a breath. "That was interesting."

"What happened?" inquired Ruth.

"In a nutshell, they wanted me to build them a cabin," said Adam. "I told them no."

Ruth raised her eyebrows. "You told them no? Why?"

"He offered to pay me very well, but they were both rude and arrogant," he concluded. "I don't want customers I can't work with, because ultimately it will backfire on me. I could tell in advance they would never be satisfied with anything I did, and all I could look forward to is bad reviews or possibly a lawsuit."

He saw her wince. "Okay, I can understand that," she said. "But is it wise to turn down a job? That's not how to grow a business."

He shook his head. "I'm only willing to grow my business under my own terms. I'm not so desperate for work that I have to take a job I know I'll regret."

"But if they were willing to pay as well as they implied, wouldn't it be worth it?"

"Nein."

"Adam, I can't help but think that was a foolish and short-sighted thing to do."

He grew irritated. "Why should I take financial advice from you?" he inquired coldly. "Isn't that what got you in trouble in the first place?"

She sucked in her breath and looked stricken.

He scrubbed a hand over his face. "Ruth, I'm sorry. I didn't mean…"

"Never mind." Her mouth trembled and she whirled around toward the kitchen door. "I'll see you tomorrow. But right now I'd better leave before I say something I'll regret." She darted outside.

"Miss Ruth!" exclaimed Lucas, who had been involved with arranging the cutlery into shapes. He stared at the door. "She didn't kiss me goodbye, *Dat.*"

Adam watched as Ruth snatched up the bicycle from where it normally leaned against a porch rail during the day. She mounted the bike and pedaled furiously down the road.

He slumped down on a kitchen chair. Why had he said something like that?

Deep down, he knew why he resented her business advice. It spoke of an interest in money and success and ambition he simply didn't share—and which was distinctly un-Amish. He understood she had an educational background in finance that he lacked, but he simply had no interest in growing beyond his ability to make a living, pay his men and raise his son.

It also made him wonder—could Ruth ever become Amish again? Or was he pinning romantic hopes on a woman who was completely ineligible?

Ruth hardly slept that night. Adam was right. Why should he take financial advice from her? She had not only lost her own money, she'd lost money for her clients. She was the last person on the planet to give financial advice.

Ambition. She saw Adam as lacking in ambition, in the drive to build his business as rapidly and comprehensively as possible, to become the biggest log-kit builder in the western half of the U.S. To earn as much money as he could.

Money. That was what it came down to.

She rolled over. She should have known better—not just because of Adam's personality, but because of his faith. Most Amish men weren't driven to succeed by the definitions of the secular world. Their perception of success was exactly like Adam's. Why couldn't she have understood that before pushing him where he wasn't interested in going?

Her financial career came back like a dark cloud to hover over her, as she lay in bed in the unlit room of the boardinghouse. The fury of her clients. The anger and disappointment of her boss.

And the lightning-bolt understanding that Wall Street was not where she belonged.

She formed one last vague thought before drifting off to sleep. Maybe it was God who had pulled her away from Wall Street and landed her here in the middle of rural Montana…

She woke the next morning determined to apologize to Adam for forcing her view of success on him. But she could still help. She could ease his burden by taking over the bookkeeping side of the business…if he was interested.

When she rode up to his farm, he stepped out on the porch to meet her. If the dark circles under his eyes were any indication, he hadn't slept any better than she had.

"Good morning," she said. "I'm here to apologize."

He gave a grim smile. "I want to apologize, too."

"I shouldn't have pushed."

"And I shouldn't have snapped."

"So we were both wrong."

"Ja." The strain went out of his face as she climbed the porch steps. "We were both wrong. I'm running a

bit late because I need to go see that couple across town, the Johnsons. We can talk it over this afternoon."

He went indoors, shouldered his satchel, kissed Lucas and departed out the back door where the horse was already hitched up to the buggy.

"Miss Ruth! Miss Ruth!" Lucas, sitting in his booster seat with a bowl of oatmeal in front of him, banged his spoon on the table.

"Good morning, little man." She dropped a kiss on his forehead. "Oatmeal? Ooh, maybe we can make oatmeal cookies this morning, what do you say?"

The rest of the day passed as so many previous days had—peacefully, calmly, with no more stress than it took to keep a rambunctious boy entertained and meals planned. Ruth took the time to deliberately savor the contrast between a typical day at her old job—pouring over spreadsheets, staring at computer screens, barking orders on the phone, pushing a client toward an investment, feeling the never-ending pressure to go go go—and a typical day here.

She and Lucas made cookies. Gathered eggs. Pulled some vegetables from the garden. Played hide-and-seek. Chatted with Nell Peachey when the older woman came to collect milk and bring by some fresh cheese.

Was this something she wanted to give up?

When Lucas went down for his afternoon nap, Ruth went into Adam's office and looked at the paperwork scattered about. Yes, she could do this. She could straighten out his muddled accounts and keep track of his finances. She could write proposals and estimates. She could do billing and payroll. In short, she could do a lot of things to keep his business solvent and productive while freeing him to do what he did best—build, create, construct, supervise.

If he agreed.

She went back into the kitchen to work on preparing dinner while Lucas napped. These goals hinged upon something she had been reluctant to face—it would mean staying beyond her original agreement to watch Lucas until Adam's autumn rush was over and winter moved in. But what then? Did she want to stay in Pierce over the winter? She knew she could always find a job in town. Was that what she wanted?

In other words, what was her *own* ambition?

The question was still unresolved when Adam came back in the late afternoon. He looked tired but more at peace than he'd been when she arrived in the morning. She suspected he had had as many internal conversations with himself as she had had within herself.

"Guder nammidaag," he said as he came in the door. Lucas bolted for him, and Adam scooped up the child in his arms. "And were you a *gut* boy for Miss Ruth today?"

"Ja! We picked tomatoes!"

"So I see." Adam eyed the pile of vegetables on the counter.

"Nell said she would can them up for you," explained Ruth, pulling a dish out of the oven.

"Ruth…" Adam hesitated. "We should talk about my very rude comment last night."

"Let's eat dinner first," she suggested. To her surprise, she felt calm and in control. "I did a lot of soul-searching last night, and if it's any comfort, I'm not nearly as upset as you might think."

After the silent blessing, while dishing up some food for Lucas, Ruth deliberately steered the conversation into neutral territory. "Tell me how the project is going with your new customers. Their name is Johnson, right?"

"Ja. It's going very well." Adam took a bite and spoke with his mouth full. "We've started cutting logs to begin the shell construction."

After dinner, Adam lifted Lucas from his booster seat. "Into the living room, *liebling*," he told the child. "Why don't you build me a nice house with your blocks while Miss Ruth and I talk?"

"Ja, Dat." The boy went out of the room.

"So first, let me apologize," he told her, leaning back in his chair and crossing one ankle over the other knee. "In light of what you told me about your background, it was incredibly rude."

She shrugged. "In the end it was probably good that you said what you did," she confessed. "I thought about it last night and realized I'm still caught up in the Wall Street mentality. Even way out here, in the middle of rural Montana, it can poison my thinking. I have to get over the notion that wealth for its own sake is something to admire, and realize ambition is a good servant but a bad master."

He looked relieved. "Then you understand why I turned down that couple that came by yesterday."

"Whether I understood or not, it isn't my business. You have your reasons. I'll admit, however, they were amazingly intrusive, treating you like a fish in a fish-bowl. I've met people like that before—arrogant, fool-ish, entitled. And to think I used to admire successful people like that—or rather, envy them." She shook her head.

"I just don't want to work with people I don't like," Adam said. "And my gut tells me they would be noth-ing but trouble in the end."

Ruth toyed with a fork. "Adam, let me ask you some-thing. Have you thought about hiring a bookkeeper or an accountant?"

He seemed surprised at the change of subject. "*Ja.* Sometimes. I have an accountant in town who does my yearly taxes, but he doesn't engage himself in the day-to-day functions of the business. I do it myself, but I'm not any good with numbers."

She leaned forward in her earnestness. "Then would you be willing to let me have a look at your books? I'm not a CPA, but I have a strong understanding of book-keeping and accounting. It—it might relieve you of a burden." She bit her lip. That almost sounded too in-timate.

He looked puzzled. "Why would you *want* to?" he blurted. "How can anyone enjoy working with num-bers?"

"We all have different gifts. I couldn't do what you're doing, building homes like you do."

"But when would you do all that bookkeeping? Your days are full with Lucas."

She fiddled with the fork. "Maybe I could work on

it after your busy season is over. My job was only supposed to last that long, wasn't it?"

He went still. "Are you saying you're not eager to leave? That you want to stay on after my season ends?"

"I'm saying it's a distinct possibility, yes." She met his eyes and saw a flare of awareness in them.

But he knew she understood the barrier between them. When he'd kissed her, she'd said it wouldn't work between them, and he knew exactly why. As a baptized member of the community, he could not breach his vows. And Ruth was not Amish.

For the first time in a long time he thought about what the bishop had said when he'd brought up that very point. He'd hinted Ruth wasn't Amish *yet*. What did the bishop see that he, Adam, didn't?

Ruth was practically *Englisch*. Adam knew the spiritual journey to become Amish was highly difficult for someone raised with modern conveniences. Yet the *conveniences* part seemed to be going well. She wasn't fazed by caring for a child in a home without electricity. She seemed eager to learn domestic skills such as canning and making cheese. She'd certainly surprised him with her ability to milk a cow.

But that was a long way from the internal journey necessary to abide by the *Ordnung*—a set of rules she hadn't grown up with, after all—and the subsuming of individual wills and desires in favor of family and community. Most of the time, this process was easy for someone raised within the church. But Ruth had been uprooted at an impressionable age, torn from her parents, raised in a foster family, educated in a worldly pursuit, and then immersed in a wildly competitive field for two years. No wonder she'd snapped.

"Let me make sure I understand," he said, as he concluded his musings. "You're willing to stay on after my busy season ends and I won't need you to watch Lucas, and you'll work on the financial side of my business?"

"In a nutshell, yes."

He hesitated a moment longer while a physical feeling of relief washed over him. Was this another answer to prayer? *"Ja,"* he said softly, and smiled.

She smiled back, her eyes dark and fathomless. "It means I won't have to leave you," she murmured.

"I'd like that," he murmured back.

The soft words belied his inner feelings. A part of him was jumping up and down with glee, not just because she would be helping with a side of his business that he was bad at, but because *she wouldn't be leaving him.* At least, not yet.

If her offer was merely an excuse to stay, he welcomed it.

Maybe *Gott* had something up His sleeve after all.

Chapter Fifteen

Alone in her room at the boardinghouse that evening, Ruth looked around. She had personalized the space as much as possible, since she didn't want to feel she was living out of suitcases. Some of her clothes hung in the closet and some were tucked inside the dresser. She had bought an inexpensive bookcase at a thrift store and used it to hold her small library. She had a few of her knickknacks scattered around. But otherwise she preferred to let the beauty of the room's Amish simplicity speak for itself. She enjoyed how the evening sun streamed through the window, lighting up the quilt and the hardwood floors.

She sat down in the rocking chair and thought about her future. Adam hadn't done backflips at her offer to take over his business dealings, but somehow she was able to read his emotions and realized her offer to stay went beyond the professional and into the realm of personal.

But what then? It wasn't like she could expect a courtship from him. She knew better. Maybe she would be better off leaving, after all.

Sighing, she picked up the Bible she had taken to reading in the evenings. The heft of the book was somehow comforting—pages and pages of spiritual guidance that had directed many people for untold generations. What kind of guidance would it offer her?

She opened the book near the beginning, and found herself in the twenty-eighth chapter of Genesis, about Jacob's search for a wife and how he left his father to find someone to marry. He vowed that if God stayed with him and provided for his needs until such time as he returned home to his father's house in safety, "then shall the Lord be my God."

She smiled. Wasn't that what had happened to her? Hadn't all her needs been provided during her wanderings? Except in her case, she had no home to return to.

She closed her eyes again and flipped ahead to another random spot, then plopped her finger on a verse. This landed her on the seventy-third Psalm. "But as for me, my feet were almost gone; my steps had well nigh slipped. For I was envious at the foolish, when I saw the prosperity of the wicked…"

She froze and felt the blood drain from her face. That was what happened to her during her job on Wall Street. She had nearly lost her foothold. She had felt envy when she saw the prosperity of the wicked.

She flipped back to Genesis, and Jacob's journey. Jacob had prayed for God to provide for his needs until he returned home, and "then shall the Lord be my God."

She leaned her head against the back of the rocking

chair and closed her eyes. Was God telling her something? Was this the home He was providing for her? *Did He want to be her God?*

Was it all falling into place?

She struggled to fall asleep that night, wrestling with what she'd read.

At long last, she drifted into a fitful sleep.

Deep in the night, she had a dream. She was a child traveling in a buggy with her mother and father, being driven by a man she somehow knew was her uncle but whose face was muted and undefinable. Her father and uncle wore black suspenders and long beards. She wore a Plain dress and apron, with a *kapp* over her hair, as did her mother.

The buggy passed fields, ditches, trees. They passed houses surrounded by cornfields and cows. The roads grew more crowded, the traffic heavier. Finally, her uncle pulled the buggy to a stop in front of a train station. She climbed down, and she and her parents pulled out a quantity of luggage from the buggy. Her parents kissed and embraced her uncle, and all had tears in their eyes.

"It's only for a little while," her uncle said. "Then you can come back."

"*Ja*, we'll be back," her father said. "This is our church. This is where *Gott* wants us to be." The dream dissolved into sadness and chaos, and Ruth woke up in tears.

She lay there, wiping the moisture from her eyes, wondering about the dream. It was the first time in a long time she had dreamt about her parents, and felt the familiar, piercing grief of their absence, a grief that had become muted and dull over time. Was God telling her through her dream that He wanted her to stay with the church of her childhood, the one her parents wanted to return to?

She didn't know. But it was an idea that took hold of her and grew in strength.

A week passed, and the idea wouldn't fade. The notion that perhaps God wanted her to return to the church of her childhood simply wouldn't go away.

"You seem thoughtful lately," remarked Adam one morning a few days later.

She and Adam had returned to a semblance of normalcy after their kiss, and were polite around each other.

She shrugged. "Just lots to think about," she prevaricated.

"Anything you can share, or is it none of my business?"

Her decision involved him to an enormous degree, but she wasn't ready to discuss it yet. Not with Adam. "Kinda none of your business," she replied. "No offense."

"None taken. I'm not one to pry."

Ruth eyed him subtly as he gathered his things and got ready to leave for work. Adam was a man of many strengths and many talents—and many admirable qualities. That was one of the things that was mixed up inside her. If she had thoughts about returning to the Amish, she had to make sure that desire was entirely separate from her interest in remaining with Adam. As Eva had pointed out, the decision to convert had to come from a spiritual foundation and not a romantic one. Otherwise it was a conversion that might not stick.

To distract her thoughts, she asked Lucas, "Are you ready to go see Miss Eva this morning? We're going to can up some carrots while you and Jacob play."

"Ja! Ja!" The boy jumped up and down and managed to bang his cast on the table. "Ow…"

"Take it easy, little man," observed Adam, hoisting the strap of his leather satchel onto his shoulder. "You don't need another broken arm." He looked at Ruth. "I'll be home at the usual time."

She nodded and busied herself with packing the carrots she intended to bring to Eva's into a spacious basket. "We'll be back long before then."

After making sure Lucas was fed, she slipped on his jacket—fortunately with sleeves wide enough to fit over his cast—and put his small straw hat on his head, then seized the basket of carrots. "Let's go!"

He skipped ahead of her down the gravel road the scant half mile to the Hostetlers'. Ruth followed at a sedate pace and took the opportunity to breathe in the sweet fall air.

Once again her mind questioned. Could she stay here? More accurately, could she leave? Ahead of her, Lucas stopped to examine a late-season flower. The child was happy, active, curious. By contrast, the children she'd known in her foster family were often traumatized, as she had been when her foster parents had first taken her in.

For the first time in a long time, she wondered what

might have happened to her if she had been placed anywhere else but with the good people who had devoted their lives to helping children in need. She stopped for a moment, closed her eyes and breathed a prayer of thanks for them.

Despite losing his mother, admittedly at too young an age to remember her, Lucas didn't suffer from that same sense of loss or deprivation. She found herself wanting to protect the boy, to guide him in the stead of a mother. But that was too permanent to think about.

Eva was out in front of her home, sweeping the walkway, with her infant tucked in a sling across her chest. *"Guder mariye!"* the young mother called.

"Guder mariye," returned Ruth. She savored the opportunity to practice the Amish language with Eva. She swung her basket. "I brought carrots!"

"And I'm ready for them in the kitchen. I have everything set up."

Lucas dashed ahead to tumble with his friend Jacob while Ruth followed Eva indoors.

The house was less steamy but just as happily chaotic. Eva's daughter Millie was busy washing jars at the sink. Eva tucked her baby into the bouncy seat on the table while Ruth lifted the basket of carrots onto a counter. The kitchen had jars, rings, lids, pressure canners, and other accoutrements of food preservation spread out and ready to use.

Ruth found she enjoyed the camaraderie of working on preserving food with Eva, with the ebb and flow of children inside and outside. Eva got one of the canners started while Ruth continued filling jars for the second canner.

When the children were outside and Eva started some water to boil for tea, Ruth posed the question that had been on her mind. With her eyes on the knife she was using to dice carrots, she asked slowly, "Eva, do you ever feel God is talking to you?"

"*Ja*, of course." The young mother looked surprised. "All the time. Why?"

"Because just recently, I've felt that way myself."

She related her dream. Eva took the whole thing in stride. "Sounds like the Holy Spirit at work," she remarked matter-of-factly. "Now your job is to listen and pay attention."

"I—I suppose." Ruth had none of Eva's unshakeable certainty. "It's all very new to me."

"But let me ask you something." The kettle started to whistle, so Eva poured out two mugs of tea, one of which she set before Ruth. "You mentioned in your dream your father said he'd be back to the church. Do you think that's what your parents planned to do? Return to the Amish?"

"I—I don't know. I think that's what is nagging me. I can't seem to get over the coincidences I've experienced in the last few weeks. What are the odds of my car breaking down outside the only Amish settlement in Montana? What are the odds Adam would rescue me and offer me a job at a time I needed a job and he needed a nanny? And if returning to the church was in my parents' plans, where does that leave me?"

"You talk about coincidences," remarked Eva with

a smile, "Are they coincidences or *Gott*'s hand?" She sipped her tea. "Now let me ask you something else. Have you thought about staying here in Montana?"

Ruth placed her mug back on the table and stared at it. "Yes," she admitted slowly. "I've thought about staying. I like this area. I like my job. It's—it's so very different than what my foster parents urged me to do—namely achieve financial independence using my business and finance education—but somehow what I've been doing lately is more viscerally satisfying. Lucas is a dear boy, and we get along very well. I could be happy here for a while. So yes, I've thought about staying."

"I can tell you someone who would be very happy if you did stay," added Eva with a small smile.

"I'm sure Lucas would be…"

"I'm not talking about Lucas. I'm talking about his father."

"I'm trying not to think about him, remember?"

"Has anything changed between you?"

Eva didn't know about that kiss, and Ruth had no intention of enlightening her. "Not really. Except it's clear we're both interested in each other but can't do anything about it. It—it's awkward at times."

"That can be fixed." A kitchen timer started beeping. Eva turned it off and got up to check the pressure canner. She nodded, turned off the heat and returned to the table. "You could return to the church. Wasn't that what your father said in your dream?"

"Th-that's kind of a big step, isn't it?" stuttered Ruth. "I was born Amish, yes, but I've lived in the *Englisch* world for fifteen years. I worked in high finance on Wall Street. Giving up all that seems enormous."

Eva cocked her head. "Forgive me if I'm stepping out of place, but it seems you've already given up all that. You haven't missed your cell phone since you lost it at that rest stop. I never see you in anything but modest clothes, so you don't seem overly interested in fashion. You've settled very nicely into a job working in a home without electricity. Would it be such a big step to give up the *Englisch* conveniences?"

"But it's so much more than that," argued Ruth. "Becoming Amish is a spiritual decision, not just a worldly one."

"Of course. But you just finished telling me a remarkable tale about how *Gott* has been providing for your needs and guiding you in so many things. Could He be guiding you to stay and join the church?"

Ruth bit her lip. "I don't know, Eva. It's such a big step."

"And a scary one, too, *ja*? But there's no rush. In fact, there shouldn't *be* a rush. But nor should you necessarily deny the possibility."

Ruth sighed. "I left behind a very complicated situation. Now it seems I'm facing bigger complications than I ever imagined."

"Sometimes that's how *Gott* works," agreed Eva. "But the rewards…" She lightly touched her baby's toes. The infant had drifted off to sleep. "…can be great."

"So what do I do next?"

"I would talk to the bishop. He's the best one to guide

you if you have questions like this. He's a *gut* man. And a wise one."

Ruth made up her mind. "I'll talk to him," she decided. "I need someone to help me figure everything out."

Chapter Sixteen

Sitting next to Eva on the women's side during church service, Ruth eyed Bishop Beiler. He was an imposing man with a full beard and gray hair, though his eyes had laugh wrinkles that indicated good humor. He spoke with power and authority. She hoped this was the man who might be able to guide her, to untangle her thoughts, to determine whether or not she should consider returning to her childhood faith. One thing was certain—she needed some spiritual counseling— and she hoped he would be the one to offer it.

In the cheerful aftermath of the service, with families and friends gathering to share a meal, Lucas came dashing over to her and she swung the child up on her hip. Adam wandered over as well. "Have you eaten yet?" he asked.

"*Nein.* But Eva invited me to sit with her and her family." She put a finger on Lucas's nose. "I'm sure you'd like to eat with your friend Jacob, *ja*?"

"Ja!" He bounced in her arms and accidentally banged his cast against her shoulder.

"Ouch. Watch yourself, little guy." Ruth looked over at Adam. "I'm sure you'd be welcome, too."

"Ja, I like the Hostetlers." She got the distinct impression he would prefer to dine with her alone, but that would be embarrassingly obvious with the community gathered around.

As she ate the midday meal with the rest of the church, Ruth wondered how she could finagle a chance to talk with the bishop about her spiritual quandary.

And then the problem solved itself. After the meal, when women were retrieving dishes and baskets and men were hitching up horses, the bishop strolled over to introduce himself.

"We haven't formally met," the bishop said, holding out a hand. "I'm Samuel Beiler."

Ruth shook his hand. "How do you do? I'm Ruth Wengerd."

"It's nice to see you at our Sunday services. Adam has told me a little bit about you."

"He has?" Startled, she glanced around, but Adam was nowhere in sight.

"Ja. He mentioned you were raised Amish, but your parents left when you were a child. Is that true?"

"Yes. I think it was supposed to be a temporary shunning. I believe my father had hopes of returning after a period of time, but my parents were killed in a car accident shortly after they left the community. I was not yet twelve years old."

The bishop shook his head. "May they rest in peace."

"Yes." Ruth gathered her courage and plunged into the topic she had been obsessing about. "Mr. Beiler, I'm glad to meet you for another reason. Can I make an appointment to speak with you? I could use some advice."

The elderly man's bushy eyebrows rose. "*Ja,* of course. Would tomorrow work?"

She hesitated. "I care for Lucas during Adam's workday. Would later this afternoon or evening be convenient?"

"*Ja,* that would work. Is it that urgent?"

She gave a wry smile. "I wouldn't call it *urgent.* More like bothersome. It's an issue I've been wrestling with for some time and would welcome the chance to discuss it with the church's spiritual leader."

He nodded. "I'd be glad to help. My home isn't too far away." He gave her directions. "How about five o'clock?"

"That would be fine. And thank you. Or should I say, *danke.*" She smiled. "My childhood language is coming back to me."

The bishop nodded and turned to join a short plump woman Ruth presumed was his wife. Ruth made her way over to Anna and Eli's buggy. She felt cautiously hopeful the bishop might be able to help resolve her dilemma.

Late that afternoon, dressed in the same sober garments she'd worn to church, Ruth set off on her bicycle for the bishop's house. She found the smallish home that looked like a made-over barn, with a large garden space up front, mostly harvested. Ruth parked the bicycle near the front door, wiped her palms down her skirt and knocked.

The same older woman she'd seen earlier answered.

"Good afternoon. You must be Ruth. My name is Lois Beiler."

"It's nice to meet you." Ruth shook hands.

Lois stepped back to allow Ruth inside. "My husband is in the back of the house where his study is. Won't you follow me?"

Ruth remembered older people usually lived in a *daadi haus* tacked on the back of a larger farmhouse, so this small stand-alone structure for a senior couple was a little unusual. She suspected it had something to do with the newness of the Amish settlement.

Lois approached an open door where the bishop was seated behind a plain wooden desk. A calico cat lay curled up on a flat cushion on the desk, sleeping. The man rose. "I'm glad to see you, Ruth. Won't you have a seat? Lois, *lieb*, please leave the door open."

Ruth knew the request had to do with maintaining propriety. Lois smiled and left the room. Ruth dropped down on a wooden chair as the older man reseated himself.

"Thank you for your time, Bishop," she began, and clasped her hands. "I—I wanted to discuss a strange issue I'm facing. First of all, do you know anything about my background?"

"Only what you told me earlier."

She told him an abbreviated version of her adolescence, young adulthood and professional failure that had sent her fleeing West, culminating in her stay in Montana.

"The more I looked at it, the more I think it was God's hand behind everything that happened. Even the blunder I made at my job—was that God pushing me away from Wall Street? I'm convinced it was God who caused me to mess up to get myself out of Wall Street before I lost my soul."

The older man nodded. "I certainly can't question your conclusion. From what you described, it seems you got very close to being caught up in an untenable situation. Being steeped in wealth like that often produces poverty of the soul."

"Yes." She pleated a fold of her skirt. "So anyway, here I am with a job I like very much, meeting people whose company I enjoy, learning tasks such as canning and cheese making that I remember my mother doing when I was very young. And now I wonder if God put me here for a reason."

"Miss Wengerd, do you know why it is your parents were under a temporary shunning?"

"They never talked about it much, at least in front of me, but I have a vague memory that my father punched a non-Amish man who was harassing my mother. He refused to feel bad about it and had something of an argument with his bishop. I think they both agreed they needed a cooling-off period, so my parents left their community."

"*Ja.* A temporary shunning is something of a special circumstance, but I can see that happening."

"The strange thing is, Bishop Beiler, I'm quite certain my parents meant to come back to the church. I don't want to be melodramatic, but I wonder if that's not what God is telling me I should be doing—returning to the church of my childhood."

The cat unfurled itself from its cushion and stepped up to the bishop, pressing her head under his chin. Absently, the bishop leaned back in his chair and pulled the cat onto his lap. An outsize purr filled the room. "Do you mean being baptized Amish?"

"Yes."

"It's a huge step," he warned.

"I know." She scrubbed a hand over her face. "But I wonder if that's what my parents wouldn't have wanted me to do."

He gave a slight shake of his head. "That's not a strong enough reason," he said. "I'm sure you're aware Amish conversions are rare for a reason, and many don't last. The only ones that do last come from a purely spiritual basis. That's what you must be sure of."

"I agree…"

"Miss Wengerd, let me ask another question. Please forgive me if this is too personal, but as the spiritual leader of our community, I feel compelled to ask. What are your feelings for Adam?"

She wasn't altogether surprised by his inquiry. "It's complicated," she confessed. "I—I won't deny there's an attraction between us. And I adore Lucas. But I'm also fully aware I shouldn't think about converting simply to pursue that interest."

To her surprise, the bishop smiled. "You're a wise woman, Miss Wengerd. It sounds like you understand very well the seriousness of what's involved in becoming baptized to our church."

"Maybe my analytical education has done some good after all." She gave him a thin smile.

He chuckled, then turned serious. "Do I understand you'll be able to continue your job watching Lucas for the foreseeable future?"

"Well, Adam said he needed me only for his busy season, basically until the snow flies. But since I have a background in finance, I offered to take over some of the business side of things, such as the bookkeeping. He seemed relieved to have someone take a hated task off his hands. We agreed the best time to do this would be during the winter months. So yes, it looks like I'm here for the foreseeable future."

He nodded. "Then, if you're serious about seeing whether you're called to become baptized, you'll need to immerse yourself as fully into the church as possible, for a long time. A year at least. It seems you're doing a fine job of remembering the language, which puts you at an advantage. You'll need to dress like an Amish woman, with a conscious effort to understand the nature and significance of the garments."

"That's fine." Ruth plucked at her blouse. "To be honest, I feel I stick out like a sore thumb dressed in *Englisch* clothes anyway. Perhaps Eva can help me sew a couple of dresses and aprons."

"And of course, if you feel the same way after immersing yourself in our community, there are five months of classes to undergo before taking the final step. Those classes will provide you with a greater understanding of the spiritual significance of a conversion. You can always leave at any time. But once a baptism happens, it's a lifelong commitment. I can't underscore that strongly enough."

She nodded. "I understand. And this will give Adam and me time to determine whether our feelings for each other are strong enough to move forward."

"Ja." The bishop's eyes twinkled. "You understand very well."

"On a more practical note…" Ruth rubbed her chin. "I might have to move out of the boardinghouse as winter approaches, since I won't be able to ride the bicycle to work each day. Eva and Daniel's home is large, and within walking distance of Adam's house. I thought I'd ask if they could rent me a room."

"If they can't, let me know and I'll find other accommodations for you."

"So—so you think I'm a good candidate to join the church?"

He smiled. "Ask me that question a year from now. But for the time being, I will welcome you at our church services and community activities."

"Thank you." Ruth stood up and held out her hand. "It's encouraging to know I'm not getting a flat refusal to convert. I will try to discern my motivation and make sure it springs strictly from a spiritual base."

The bishop shook her hand, his grip firm and hearty. "I can't predict where the Lord will lead you," he remarked, "but it would not surprise me if you were to end up joining the church. Please, don't hesitate to let me know if you have any more questions."

"Thank you. Lovely cat, by the way."

The bishop stroked the animal's fur. "We have a long and unusual history with this little lady. She taught me much about the grievous sin of pride. It's one of the reasons I'm willing to consider you as a member of our church. It's a story I might tell someday, but not now."

Puzzled by such a cryptic comment, and with much to think about, Ruth left the bishop's house and headed back to town.

Adam finished the silent blessing at dinner on Monday afternoon. It had been a long day of work and he was tired—and grateful to Ruth. Again and again he came home to find the house tidy and welcoming, his son happy, and a hot meal on the table. His prayer had much to do with his appreciation of the woman sitting opposite him.

As for the future—well, he had decided to leave it in *Gott*'s hands. There was little he could do about it anyway.

Ruth unfolded Lucas's napkin for him and edged his cup of milk closer within the child's reach. "I had a talk with the bishop yesterday afternoon."

He froze, his fork suspended in midair. His heart started thumping. "You did? Why?" He recalled the bishop's visit after Lucas broke his arm, when the church leader all but gave his blessing on a match between himself and Ruth—under one condition.

But a lifetime of restraint kept him from asking what happened at the meeting. Asking about someone's spiritual status—it just wasn't done. Everyone's religious journey wasn't worn on the sleeve; it was a close personal matter.

But why would Ruth seek out the bishop? What did they discuss?

She met his eyes over the width of the table, and there was a spark of humor in their dark depths. "Don't you want to know what we discussed?"

"Ja," he croaked. "But you don't have to tell me. It's none of my business."

"I wouldn't have brought it up if I thought it was none of your business." She picked up her fork but merely toyed with her food. "I went to see him because I wanted to discuss some things with him." She kept her eyes on her plate. "I can't help but feel God has been leading my life to this point. So I—I asked Bishop Beiler if it was possible for me to become Amish."

Adam closed his eyes and breathed a prayer of thanksgiving. If this wasn't *Gott* working a miracle right in front of him, he didn't know what was. He reopened his eyes. His voice was still hoarse. "And what did the bishop say?"

"He said the impulse to convert had to come from a purely spiritual source. And—and he said it could not be influenced by any attraction between us."

Adam felt his own spark of humor arise. "Smart man, that bishop," he murmured.

"Yes. This won't be a fast process, Adam. I need to immerse myself in the community for a year, dress properly, and of course take the classes leading up to baptism." She held out both hands, palms up.

He took her hands in his. "The span of time will serve two purposes," he told her. "It will discern whether you're right for the church, and it will discern whether we're right for each other."

She gave a shaky laugh. "That's right…"

"Why are you holding hands?" asked Lucas in a puzzled voice.

Adam chuckled and released Ruth's grip. "Because Miss Ruth and I are good friends. You like Miss Ruth, don't you Lucas?"

"Ja!" The child banged his fork on the table, apparently aware of something significant in the air and willing to enter the discussion with enthusiasm. "She plays games with me and reads me stories. I want her to stay here forever."

"I think," said Adam, his eyes twinkling, "that's a *gut* enough reason to keep her around a bit longer." His heart soared with hope and optimism.

"And I think," added Ruth, dropping a kiss on top of Lucas's head, "that's a good reason for me to stay, too." She smiled at Adam, a smile full of promise of what the future might bring.

Epilogue

Ruth watched as her new stepson, Lucas, and his friend Jacob dashed outside to play in the crisp November weather, soon after her and Adam's wedding ceremony, which had happened only two days after her baptism.

"How does it feel to be Mrs. Chupp?" inquired Adam, slipping an arm around her waist as he sidled up beside her.

She leaned into him for a moment, then pulled away, knowing public displays of affection were discouraged among the Amish. "Wonderful," she breathed. "Not only do I get to keep being Lucas's mother, but I get to be your wife. I've tried to figure out which one I like better, and it's a tough choice."

"You didn't make vows to Lucas," he joked. "You made vows to me."

Her eyes crinkled as she smiled up at him. "You're right. That makes it easy." She had to resist the urge to fling her arms around his neck. "I'm the luckiest woman alive. I get to stay with you forever!"

"And here I thought it was just a convenient business arrangement." He chuckled. "You're doing all the company finances anyway."

"Hey, that's right." She winked at him. "You're definitely getting the better end of the deal. A wife *and* an employee."

He pulled her closer and against decorum, Ruth gave into her impulse to hug her new husband. "I love you, husband."

Adam hugged her back. "I love you, wife. For now and forever."

* * * * *

Dear Reader,

I've often wondered how hard it would be to land on one's feet after everything goes awry. Here's the story of a young woman whose life goes haywire, and lives to tell the tale.

I'm partial to nanny stories because our older daughter was a nanny for many years—a certified, professional nanny, in fact, graduate of a nanny school. She's in a different field now, but loves working with children.

When most people think of Montana, they think of cowboys and ranches and wide-open spaces. There are plenty of these, but there's another side to this vast and beautiful state as well—such as small isolated towns with their own stories to tell. The mythical town of Pierce is based on the town nearest to where we live, with a similar cast of characters. Art reflects reality, as they say.

In populating the Amish settlement outside of Pierce, I referenced characters from my last book, *The Amish Animal Doctor*. I also look forward to setting future stories in this beautiful location.

I love hearing from readers and welcome emails at patricelewis1305@mail.com.

Blessings,
Patrice

HER AMISH ADVERSARY
Indiana Amish Market • by Vannetta Chapman

Bethany Yoder loves working at her father's outdoor Amish market, but when he hires Aaron King to help out, Bethany and Aaron don't see eye to eye about anything. She wants to keep things the same. He's all for change. Can opposites ever attract and turn to love?

THE AMISH BACHELOR'S BRIDE
by Pamela Desmond Wright

Amish widow Lavinia Simmons is shocked to learn that her late husband gambled away their home. Desperate to find a place for herself and her daughter, she impulsively accepts bachelor Noem Witzel's proposal. A marriage of convenience just might blend two families into one loving home.

DEPENDING ON THE COWBOY
Wyoming Ranchers • by Jill Kemerer

Rancher Blaine Mayer's life gets complicated when his high school crush, Sienna Powell, comes to stay with her niece and nephew for the summer. Recently divorced and six-months pregnant, Sienna takes his mind off his ranch troubles, but can he give her his heart, too?

BOUND BY A SECRET
Lone Star Heritage • by Jolene Navarro

After his wife's murder, Greyson McKinsey seeks a fresh start in Texas with his twin girls in the witness protection program. When he hires contractor Savannah Espinoza to restore his barns, his heart comes back to life. But can he ever trust her with the truth?

TOGETHER FOR THE TWINS
by Laurel Blount

When Ryder Montgomery assumes guardianship of his out-of-control twin nephews, he flounders. So he enlists the help of a professional nanny. Elise Cooper quickly wins the boys' hearts—and their uncle's admiration. One sweet summer might convince the perpetual bachelor to give love and family a try...

RESCUING HER RANCH
Stone River Ranch • by Lisa Jordan

Returning home after losing her job, Macey Stone agrees to care for the daughter of old friend Cole Crawford. When Macey discovers Cole is behind a land scheme that threatens Stone River Ranch, will she have to choose between her family's legacy and their newfound love?

HARLEQUIN
PLUS

Announcing a **BRAND-NEW** multimedia subscription service for romance fans like you!

Read, Watch and Play.

Experience the easiest way to get the romance content you crave.

Start your **FREE 7 DAY TRIAL** at
<u>www.harlequinplus.com/freetrial</u>.